SOLDIERS
IN HIDING

SOLDIERS
IN HIDING

A novel by
RICHARD WILEY

The Atlantic Monthly Press
BOSTON / NEW YORK

FIRST EDITION

LIBRARY OF CONGRESS CATALOGING-IN-PUBLICATION DATA

Wiley, Richard.
   Soldiers in hiding.

   I. Title.
PS3573.I433S65   1986   813'.54   85-22916
ISBN 0-87113-046-7

"Mood Indigo" by Ellington, Mills, Bigard. Copyright 1931 by
Mills Music, Inc. Copyright renewed. All rights reserved. Used
with permission.

A poem of Bashō from *The Narrow Road to the North and Other Travel
Sketches* by Bashō, translated by Nobuyuki Yuasi (Penguin Classics,
1966), copyright © Nobuyuki Yuasi, 1966. Reprinted by permission
of Penguin Books, Ltd.

"Nansen Cuts the Cat in Two" from *Zen Flesh, Zen Bones*, by Paul
Reps. Reprinted by permission of Charles E. Tuttle Co., Inc.,
Tokyo.

MV
Published simultaneously in Canada

PRINTED IN THE UNITED STATES OF AMERICA

PART ONE

ONE

IT gives me pleasure to hinder American tourists occasionally. It is a small pleasure, to be sure, but a real one, and it is so very un-Japanese.

There was a woman recently who stood at the edge of the street next to the mouth of an open subway, waiting for an obliging stranger, for someone to stop and ask if he might be of help. Her husband stood with her wearing slacks of many colors, the kind that stretch a little and hug the knees.

When I came into the dim morning they were facing me, so I smiled and heard the woman say, "Ask this man, dear. Older men are often the most accommodating."

She put five sausage fingers between his shoulder blades and gave him a little nudge, a small push in my direction. Salary men in grays and browns hurried by all around us, for as is my custom I had been the first off the train and now my coriders were catching up, coming out into a grim daylight of their own.

"Excuse me," said the man, even then standing a little aside so that I could see his big wife nodding a few feet behind him. "Do you speak English?"

I smiled, leading him out of the pedestrian flow, over against a wall where we could talk more privately.

"We're looking for Tokyo Tower," he told me. "We want to go there."

He spaced his words slowly and evenly so I cocked my head a little and looked at him, at the smiling face of his wife over his shoulder.

"To-ki-yo Tow-er," he said again, lips narrowing.

"I understand," I told him.

The wife was pulled to us by streams of people heading, now, into the station. "He speaks English, Harold," she told her husband. "We've found one with good English." She turned to me and said, "We're from Des Moines. He's been here before."

"Sure has changed," he said.

I looked at them both a second and behind them, through the low smog, I could actually see Tokyo Tower a little, coming like a dunce cap off the small broadcast station that was my own destination.

"You've got to take the train," I told them. "You must go deep down into this station and take the Ginza line. Take it as far as it will go. The last stop is right at the foot of Tokyo Tower."

"My," said the wife. "I didn't realize we were so far."

This little anecdote, this little meanness, is exemplary of my state of mind these days. The man was my junior by less than a decade. Fewer than ten years separated his plump face from my drawn one, from my thin Japanese face with its lines and folds, yet they saw me as old. And his wife with the color of her hair actually entering the realm of blue. With people such as these it is easy to be deceitful. It is easy to be mean to men whose pants stretch about the knees, whose pants are multicolored, who waggle for their wives so. Indeed, my false finger took pleasure in pointing and it was beyond me to simply say, "I'm going that way

4

myself," and to take them to the tower, to the sale of all its cheap replicas with which they might decorate Des Moines.

*

THE name of my television program is the "Original Amateur Hour"; does that ring a bell? You may have heard of another one by the same name. I start the show and end it with a rendition of "Mood Indigo," for in the early fifties that was the tune that propelled me to fame. In the beginning I limited my "Amateur Hour" strictly to serious acts, to the playing of musical instruments, to singing and dancing, and to impersonators. Now, however, it is novelty that wins the day. A woman can win, as one did last month, because of an ability to lift her lower lip up over the bridge of her nose without the use of her hands.

The "Amateur Hour" was very successful after the war. The thoroughness of our defeat was manifested in our new idea of entertainment, in the flavor of our music, and in our dress as well. I had extreme popularity for I was one of the few Japanese who spoke perfect English, and I knew the ways of America perfectly. In the early days of my "Amateur Hour" it was the impersonators of Americans who were the great successes. The country could be moved to laughter so easily then.

Now I am alone in my projection room, watching and editing a tape of the program as it will be broadcast soon. The logo, TEDDY MAKI'S ORIGINAL AMATEUR HOUR, lifts and floats from view and I come onstage. I have my guitar with me and sit on a high stool all alone on the stainless-steel stage floor. I say everything first in English, then in Japanese, and when I make a joke the laughs of old dead audiences come out of their cans and echo across the room. I play my introductory tune, then stop abruptly to read from the English language cue card that bobs by the camera. I can't read Japanese well, so when the joke is in that language it must be printed in Roman characters eight inches high. My old face bends to the work of the guitar, then looks deep into the camera's eye. My phrasing is impeccable, the tune is my trademark. "Mood Indigo" — so perfectly mannered, so properly manicured for a man of such soft delivery as mine.

There is a shift after a commercial to another camera angle and there I am again, this time ready to introduce the first guest. I stop the reel with the buttons on the arm of my chair and for a moment sit in the dark. I see only the red glow of the cigarette that I am holding, burning in front of my face. I wonder, do the people from Des Moines still ride the long subway under the city? When the next good citizen directs them correctly, will they perhaps try to find me? Will they wish for a confrontation? Or perhaps, exhausted and saddened in their hot hotel, they will turn on the television and there I'll be, the enemy before them. . . .

The projector is on again, shifting from my old face and settling softly on a seven-year-old girl, her eyes wide and waiting for the first strains of her music. As she does her folk dance the camera lights on me and then back to the little girl in time to catch her stumbling on the edges of her new gown. I introduce some others, a woman who can contort, a man who can drink water through his nose, but the last guest turns out to be the winner for he is a farter and farters are in vogue this year. The man, gray like the subway riders, wears a Rotary pin in his lapel and stands erect. He claims to be able to play tunes with his gas and says he will demonstrate by letting the television audience hear the first two bars of my theme song. We laugh together and I stand up to the man who bends over neatly, his well-tailored ass round and polite toward the camera. . . . "Mood

Indigo" is barely discernible in the mournful sound that he makes.

When I turn the lights off again and listen, I can hear the rest of the show turning onto the pickup reel, slapping lightly at the back of the room. I edit every show as haphazardly as I've done this one, choosing the acts according to how distasteful they are. The farter rolls around behind me on the end of the celluloid, smiling out at the audience with each turn, and the little folk dancer must go back to the countryside and try to explain why she didn't make it and the farter did. She would not understand, but I must push toward the collapse of culture in the remaining years that I have. It is not for me to let such little girls carry Japan any farther forward on her old wheels. Here in the dark with the white glow of the dying screen in my eyes, I can imagine as I will an "Amateur Hour" that once again takes the hearts of my adopted countrymen by storm. I have even thought that perhaps, if I could find my man from Des Moines again, I would recruit him, ask him to come on the air and sing the songs that I remember from my youth. Maybe he would sing of World War II, as if his Japanese audience, sitting softly on their *zabuton*, had somehow shared the same wartime music, held the same memories, carried the same victories in their aging hearts.

But enough. I am a figure of waning prominence, it is true, but my name is permanently lodged in the memories of nearly all my countrymen. Teddy Maki. Teddy Maki. The name has a certain ring to it, don't you agree? The way those final vowels lift it so nicely into Japaneseness.

*

WHEN I was a child life was wonderful. In the city there was a small grocery store full of vegetables, fruit, and soft fresh fish. In the valley there was a farm, Maki's farm. My uncle and father served each other well, for all of the children of both men worked the farm in late spring and summer and then spent the other seasons living above the grocery and going to school. For a while we had tried attending school in the valley near our home, but the long stares of the other children quickly sent my brothers and me toward the city and the tolerance of numbers. In the part of Los Angeles where my uncle kept his store it was possible to see kimonoed men and women and to hear only Japanese for days.

It is interesting to remember, to try to recall, the first realization one has of being different. During my early years the color of people, the curve of an eye, the texture of hair, the height and prominence of a cheekbone were all invisible to me. But as I grew older they came into focus. *We* stayed together in our small and studious way while *they* fanned out across the world. I remember a time, before my father had saved enough money to buy his farm, when he made his living as a gardener, trimming and pruning the bushes of our neighbors. He would often take me with him on his jobs, letting me ride high atop the clippings in the back of his truck, and he would laugh at the half-understood insults that sometimes came his way. On Saturdays, during those years, our family practice was to go to town together and to shop and walk along the boarded streets as if they were our own. My mother's dress, the way it hung so oddly long, made her legs look like cucumbers, and my father's hat was always tight across his eyes. Why, I remember thinking, did they need to be so strange? The parents of other children were all belt buckles and boots, all muscular and tall, yet my father, even from the low vantage point of his son's eyes, was clearly the smallest of men. What boy, under such circumstances, wouldn't long for Los Angeles? To have an uncle such as mine seemed like a gift from the gods, and the longer I stayed with him, the farther I grew from my father, the more impossible it became to go back.

Once, when I was in the tenth grade and had been staying with my uncle for three or four years, a girl, her very existence couched in blonds and blues, fell in love with me and chose several paths by which I might walk her home from school. The girl's name was Trudy, Germanic and pure, and her hair had ringlets which would bounce when she walked so tall beside me. I can remember waiting in the alley behind her house, knee-deep in the grass and hidden by the dusk. When she could sneak away Trudy would run to me. In the alley behind her house she would remove her jacket and pull my willing head in between her giant breasts, in among the white walls of flesh that moved past my ears. She talked to me in a low voice, asking me if I liked it and what I wanted to do, but when she pulled my head back all I could do was gasp, panting for air, until she laughed and plugged my mouth with one of her huge nipples, making me dizzy and helpless once again.

After the war came and when I wondered at the ironies in my life I often thought of Trudy. She would have given herself to the war effort, I knew, but would she have considered the Japanese dangerous? Remembering my thin body in her arms she would probably have thought us weak and said that it was the Germans who were the real worry, for the blood in their veins was in hers. Still, whenever I search my memory for signs of Los Angeles I find Trudy first, for she is that part of which, at the time, I was most proud. As I grew older I wanted less and less to spend my summers picking fruit and vegetables on my father's farm. My uncle, with the city behind him, grew toward America so much faster than Father. His English was better and his humor was ruled, like my own, by what he heard on the radio, by what was new. Progressively each year, when school was out, the features of the farm became less appealing, my father's form more foreign. When he, in his tired old truck, would stop at the store, and when we heard him talking to my uncle below, my cousins and I would look at each other or out the window at Los Angeles and yearn for the summer we'd miss, for the time when the parks and nearby beaches would be full, when young Japanese girls, as well as many others, would be waiting. Nevertheless, it took me until the summer after graduation to insist that I would no longer go, that I was educated now and would find my future in music, that I'd stay in Los Angeles and live above my uncle's store like a real American boy.

My cousins and brothers, all younger than myself, were packed into the pickup and gone, and suddenly the upper floor of my uncle's store, with its outside staircase leading to the open city, was mine alone. Where was Trudy, I remember wondering, when I needed her most? Now that I was a graduate she was two years gone and had moved across the city to Hollywood. She'd called a time or two, late at night, but she couldn't get past my uncle's English, and the telephone was forever in his domain. So with the place to myself I really did turn my attention to my talent. A guitar sat across my lap hours each day and, true to the Japanese stereotype, I could copy anything. I listened to recordings of the Ellington band and in a while could play rhythm or do wild solos, note for note, with whoever was on the record. My uncle used to come quietly up and sit on the edge of one of the six beds in the room and listen. . . . "Teddy, Teddy," he would sometimes say, smiling.

In my high school class there were others who played, and on the Fourth of July we did a dance, our first job. It was a block party held at a hall near my uncle's store, and we were beside ourselves with the success of it. My uncle marveled at the way we sounded so professional, and my cousins, home from the farm for the holiday, stood in stupid silence at the side of the room. They all said, "Is that Teddy up there? Is that our Teddy?"

The leader of the band was a boy my age whose name was Jimmy Yamamoto. Jimmy was dark of mood and walked around the neighborhood with his hands deep in his pockets, a soulful look on his face. He was from a broken home, something nearly unheard-of among Japanese immigrants of that day, and it had been rumored throughout the high school that for a time Jimmy was in trouble with the law. He was a thin man, unmuscular and smooth, yet there was an aura about him which made the rest of us feel something akin to fear. He spoke so little, had no need of friends, seemed to know so much.

Nevertheless, it was Jimmy Yamamoto's ability at booking that meant everything to the band. When he spoke to people he kept his voice low, but there was something about his manner that made them listen. By the end of the summer, when my cousins came back, Jimmy had acquired the habit of standing around the store, silently peeling himself a peach, and staring at the steady customers. My uncle and I felt a little proud that he had adopted us, though we had no idea why.

"He's done more for the band than you have," my uncle said one night, nodding toward Jimmy at the back of the store. "Why don't you ask him to name it?"

"It has a name already," said Jimmy, not coming forward but somehow getting his voice all the way up front to us.

"What do you think, Jimmy?" asked my uncle. "Some nice catchy name. Something that will bring pride to the neighborhood."

Jimmy stopped leaning on the long meat counter and walked slowly up to where my smiling uncle stood.

"We're going to call the band 'Jimmy Yamamoto and the American Japs,' " he said.

My uncle didn't move. A smile lingered at the edges of his mouth. "What?" he said.

"That's what I want to call the band."

My uncle and I looked at each other. I knew Jimmy wasn't joking though I'd never heard the name before, but my uncle wasn't sure. "You want to call the band, 'American Japs'?" he asked, his voice still uncommitted.

Jimmy nodded, smiling slightly, but my uncle's smile was gone. "You can't do it," he said.

"It's a good name," said Jimmy. "I've given it a lot of thought and it is a name with distinction, one that will be difficult to forget."

"It is a bad name," said my uncle. "It calls attention to prejudice rather than pride. It will make the community ashamed rather than knit it together."

"It's a good name," said Jimmy.

"A bad one," said my uncle.

The argument over the name of the band went on like this for days, my uncle furiously thinking up better names when Jimmy was gone, then hitting him with them when he came in sometime after dark.

"Anything else," he said, finally. "The community wants this band to work but not with that name. Anything else, Jimmy, and you can take the town by storm and with our blessing. What do you say? Choose another name?"

Jimmy had his trumpet tucked under his arm. He carried in his hand a list of jobs stretching to Christmas. "Look at the bookings," he told us. He left the list with my uncle and then walked away.

"He's a good boy," my uncle told me. "What did I tell you? I knew it all the time." He swung the booking list in my direction. "Trumpet players are always the leaders," he said, remembering for a moment whose uncle he was.

"He's calling the band 'Jimmy and the Ayjays'; what do you think? A reasonable compromise, don't you agree?"

The essence of Jimmy Yamamoto, so far as I could tell, was contained in the name that he first chose for our band. Jimmy Yamamoto and the American Japs. Irreverence. He was a man I was awed by and I could never understand why he wanted me for a friend. I was simple and standard for my age, while Jimmy was smart and cool. The only time I was his equal was when we played. His trumpet and my guitar were friends of the first order, and though the other members of the band came and went, it was always Jimmy and I who were steadfast.

For six months we played jobs every weekend. During the week I would go back to my uncle's store to hang about with my younger cousins, listening to talk of the high school, of what it had been like on the farm that summer. My father believed my uncle when he told him what a good musician I was, and even my mother, silent as always, came to wonder about her eldest son. Was it such a fine idea to give up a chance for college? She asked my uncle and he answered by saying, "Why don't you go hear them?" He took her by the shoulders as he said it. "Why not?" he asked. "Why not go listen to the band play?"

But though we gave them several opportunities, my parents never came to hear the band. My mother took my uncle's word, believing blindly that I had talent, and my poor father laughed when he heard what Jimmy'd wanted to call the band. They were from Japan, those parents of mine, and they'd rebuilt that world in east Los Angeles and the San Fernando Valley. I knew my parents could never be American, no more than I could ever be Japanese. "Why don't you call the band 'American Japanese'?" my father suggested, and we all laughed. My uncle put his hands upon my father's head, roughing him up gently, as an elder brother would. My father was a farmer, not a merchant; we all knew that. He was interested in the old things like *shamisen* and Noh. It had been a long time since I, or any of the others in the family, had taken him seriously or listened to the things he said.

*

WHEN I finish at the studio it is often too early for anything but the long trip home or for a visit to my son in his terraced mansion all surrounded by his wealth. Today, however, it seems to have taken me longer than usual to reduce the "Amateur Hour" to its lowest common denominator, to the farters and contortionists who keep it toward the tops of the charts. From the studio it is a slow walk, for a man my age, to Roppongi, which is always my evening destination. My mistress, a woman I have kept for three years now, has a small business, which I set up for her on one of the narrow Roppongi streets that slip back off the main one. My mistress's name is Sachiko, and the bar that she manages is called the Kado. She is in her late thirties so she remembers the war, but with the wide warp of her child's memory, that is all. She is from Hiroshima and has dull scars, the shadows of bomb burns, on her arms and thighs and belly. Sachiko's spirit is light, her laugh easy. Yet it seems to me that she is connected as I am, fused by the very blanching of her skin, to the life and technology of North America. It is for this reason that I want her. It is in her hurt that I find safe harbor, though I have a wife at home who would gladly give the same.

In Tokyo the low winter clouds push down upon shops and restaurants, making me hurry. In Roppongi daylight leaves early and as I walk, unobserved, I pass through parts of the city that are pleasing to me. I walk for a while among cement girders, heavy highways held up by them, and the roar of traffic cast down upon the road beside me. This cement coating is what lets the country wear so well, the cloth that keeps it clean. Soon there is a side street I can enter, which takes me out of all the traffic and gives me old Japan. Here there are geisha houses behind high mauve walls, their privacy protected. Sachiko's bar is not among these, yet it is here that she first thought to rise. The geisha, all white-faced and riding down the cobblestones in her jinrikisha, is still a mighty myth among failed bar girls.

On a corner, at the nearest edge of main Roppongi, I can see the Kado's neon sign, dull but brightening in the gray dark. Behind it many other such signs are coming into their own, for we are not far from a wide street where westerners go to drink, not far from plastic-looking British-style pubs where red-rouged Japanese girls go to try to find husbands, or if that's too harsh, simply to live a little. "Hello," I say to someone. *"Konbanwa. . . ."* It is barely eight o'clock, but the banter and business of running the bars is started.

The door to the Kado is opened a foot by a bright bucket of wash water sandwiched against its jamb. Inside it is dark, but Hanachan, Sachiko's bartender, is there, cleaning glasses and tidying up.

"Oi, Hana, Sachiko's not in yet?"

He turns and glares in his nightly way, then laughs. "Teddy Maki!" he shouts. "Your show will be on soon. Let's turn up the TV!"

Hanachan pulls a big bottle off the shelf, sets it on the bar, and says, "Sachiko's down the street visiting. Do you want me to go for her?"

"Keep the goddam television turned down," I tell him. "Let Sachiko come back when she's ready. You're a nosy little twerp, Hana; how old are you now?"

It is this kind of banter that whiles away the early hours every night. Hanachan is twenty-five but when I ask him his age he adds a few years and replies smartly. He is a senser of moods, this man, and knows when to be playful and when to leave me alone. It is now, in the early evening, that he thinks me most dangerous. He says my mean streak is what is natural but that booze brings out my best.

A group of customers pulls open the door and Hana hurries to take the bucket out of their way and to greet them. "Welcome," he says. "You're in the Kado. Make yourselves comfortable; our selection is meager but we aim to please."

There are only ten seats at the bar, only a few tables and booths, but now that one of them is taken Sachiko appears, her white kimono shining as it's silhouetted there in the closing sliver of street.

"Ah, gentlemen," she says, stern with herself for having had Hana greet them. "That you have stayed does us honor. Sorry for the slow start. Hanachan, bring these gentlemen drinks, bring *otsumami*, hurry!"

Sachiko sees to it that the three men are seated, then slides in next to the one who sits alone. "Working late?" she asks. "What company are you with?"

In the mirror behind the bar I can see her, but though she knows I am here she will not greet me; she'll stay with the customers, letting them sing her the praises of their company, sometimes letting one she likes or one who insists swing his arm down under the table to rest his hand upon the folds of her gown. In the mirror, warped as it is, the bottles that line its ledge take on odd proportions, are oddly magnified, the levels of liquor seeming higher. And Sachiko's arms, coming like graceful tongues from the mouths of her kimono sleeves, are also enlarged by the poor workmanship of the glass. Is it a stain or can I actually see the edge of a shining scar as she pours more booze for the businessmen?

As I look toward the door two figures walk in, then step up behind me and put their hands on my shoulders. It is my son, Milo, and his driver, Junichi.

"Father," Milo says, "we've found you at last."

Milo has a penchant for silly statements such as this. He always knows where I am if he wants me. Junichi is wearing his chauffeur's uniform and standing at attention. He is one of Milo's childhood friends but recently has cut his hair and fashioned himself into a radical, a member of Japan's New Right.

"What do you want, Milo?" I ask. "I thought you were staying in tonight. Has something happened? Is something wrong?"

Though Milo has come to the Kado for me before, he always sends Junichi in to fetch me while he waits in the long back seat of his big car. Milo's never really met Sachiko, and though he would never say so, he doesn't like the idea of her. He prefers to keep a balanced memory of his mother and me, though I'm sure he knows that my heart is sometimes away from home.

Milo is awkwardly expansive. "I'm taking Junichi down the street for a drink," he says. "It is his birthday and I'm telling him that tonight he is not allowed to wait in the car. Come. Help me make him celebrate."

Junichi is always dead quiet, but I like him for it. He has marvelous posture and, in his silences, I am able to imagine a certain pride and restraint that Milo usually lacks. Still, I would not leave the Kado so soon after arriving if customers were not usurping Sachiko's time, my time with her. But I have not seen my son now for more than a week. I stand and look at Sachiko for a moment, sitting with her group of guests, but she is so busy playing bar games that she does not notice. When Hana sees me, he comes quickly around the bar and bows, opening the door for us. The cold outside air makes him wince. . . . "Bye-bye," he says, waving.

Milo's car is longer than it should be, and wider. In the back seat he has most of the amenities of a home, but tonight we all sit in the front. Milo appears to want something special from Junichi, a rekindling of their earlier camaraderie, perhaps, though Junichi is miles from Milo now and is loyal to him without all that. We are only going a few blocks, so Junichi turns the big car around and then immediately begins to look for a parking place. Milo is sitting in the middle and nudges me once in an animated way. "He's actually younger than I am," he says, foolishly. "Would you believe it? He acts so old."

Though we are very close to Sachiko's, the street, in the direction we are going, is far busier. Milo spots a parking place right in front of his favorite bar and proudly points it out to Junichi. "Here!" he says. "What luck! What luck!" He wants to give the parking place to Junichi, another birthday present for his chauffeur.

Milo's favorite bar is very elegant, with long leather lounge chairs and real roses in the washrooms. When we get out of the car I notice two tall foreigners leaning against a set of motorcycles parked up next to the building. They hold their helmets tight against their stomachs, under their jackets, like hard pregnancies. They are speaking English and one of them is demanding something from the other. They speak roughly and with abandon, assuming anonymity, willing to say anything about anybody.

"Look at the size of that car," one of them says. "Look at the jerk driving it."

There is a line of people waiting to enter the bar but Milo waves his hands and soon we are inside. We are quickly taken upstairs and shown to a table, poor Junichi still standing stiff, here because he's told to be, nothing more. Milo orders several bottles of champagne, then excuses himself and goes off around the room shaking hands with important people. He's got very long hair and the blue jeans that he constantly wears have holes in them. He is as surely in uniform as his chauffeur in his dark and braided suit, though

I'd wager he'd deny it. . . . I lift my mood above Junichi's and speak to him.

"Well, Jun, when was the last time we drank together? How old are you now? What birthday is this?"

He chooses the last two of my questions and answers lowly. "I am thirty-seven. It is my thirty-seventh."

Junichi's entire weight rests upon the first four inches of his big chair. He carries himself like a military man, filling the contours of his uniform properly.

"That is a good age for politics," I tell him. "A good age for strong beliefs. When I was thirty-seven too much had happened to me for such luxuries. I was jaded young."

Junichi's downcast eyes do not hide well his disdain for the stories of old men. There is no humor in him — that's one problem — no love for such decadence as this bar allows. I do not resist the urge to pick on him.

"Are you still a practicing politician, Jun? A believer in the Imperial way?"

"It is not proper, sir, to discuss it here."

"But surely," I say, "Japan was a power once. She can be so again."

As soon as I speak I regret it, for Junichi will not answer. With Milo I have cultivated a tendency toward teasing, but Junichi is unconnected to all of that. He is outside my sphere of influence and if I am to tease him it must be in subtler ways.

"Listen," I say, taking a ten-thousand-yen note from my pocket and placing it before him. "Excuse me, will you? I don't believe in anything political myself, but please accept this birthday gift. Think of it as a donation."

I place the note carefully on the table, where it rests upon the polished brim of his chauffeur's cap. I am anxious to see the actual act of Junichi picking it up and putting it into his pocket, for such an act will defy his disdain, his aloofness and formality. I know he needs the money, but if he takes it I will grin widely at him and he will know that he has lost.

The champagne has arrived and Milo is opening it before I fully realize that he is back. Junichi is smiling oddly at the money and Milo is newly determined to show his belief in equality. It isn't a very Japanese endeavor and I fear that he must have inherited it from me. All Junichi wants is to be left alone by Milo, to drive my son's big car, and, perhaps, to dream of victories for the New Right.

"Now," says Milo, "forgive my disappearance." He is looking directly at Junichi and smiling, but his words carry the distinct cadence of a command and I wonder if Junichi and my son have been having a quarrel. He slides two full glasses of champagne easily across the table, making a path through the few drops that he has spilled. He picks up a third glass and holds it above his head, making me fear, for a moment, that he might include the whole room in his toast.

"To Junchan," he says. He looks at his chauffeur with misting eyes. "To his future and to the fulfillment of his desires."

I do not want to sit here under the influence of Milo's mood all evening, but that crisp new bill is still resting against his chauffeur's cap. Under normal circumstances Milo does not speak so much to Junichi, and I can see that he is having trouble holding things together now. He is smiling hard but can think of nothing more to say. When Milo proposed his toast Junichi had put the brimming glass to his lips, but he didn't drink. Milo, on the other hand, continues to pour furiously, filling my glass and his own. There are three bottles in the ice bucket and I fear we'll have to drink them all.

We sit quietly for a very long time, and as we do so a small group of Milo's fans form a semicircle around the table. They all carry napkins in their hands, some of them holding pencils up, trying to catch my son's eye. Both Junichi and I view them happily. We've been granted a momentary reprieve.

As the fans move in, the chauffeur and I push our big chairs slightly back. Milo is very good with fans. He likes them and will take whatever time is necessary to please them all. They bend around him, asking questions, laughing easily at anything Milo wants to say. He puts his champagne glass to one young woman's lips. She drinks greedily, bending farther down over my son.

Junichi's posture and position at the table have been constantly visible to me, but as I look now I see that the money is no longer resting on the brim of his cap. How could he have pocketed it and yet maintained his stiff posture, his formality? Though there are fans everywhere he takes the trouble to glance through the forest of human limbs between us and to look directly into my eyes. There is no mockery in his face, nothing changed, no lessening of his aloofness or increase in his disdain. Only Junichi knows whether the money is folded darkly inside his uniform pocket or crumpled under the belt of a thief.

With the money gone and all this silliness raging around me I have no more energy to stay. Already it is late and I have stayed too long. I push my chair back, standing. Milo and his fans are in a kind of choral repose, all smiling and swaying. Junichi's hollow eyes follow me so I bow, letting him know that I respect the small defeat he has given me. He bows back but his blue uniform works like a spring, returning him quickly to his upright position.

On the stairs that lead down to the bar's entrance is a group of middle-aged foreigners, their Japanese host telling them that their table will be ready soon. They're speaking English and thinking up nice things to say about Japan, yet I am too tired and have no time for them, no tricks on hand. I am willing to simply sidle past, but one, from their number, claws at my arm, attaching himself firmly to my elbow.

"Hey, buster," he says, and I turn to the dismal eyes of the man from Des Moines.

"Oh hello," I say, trying to smile. This is not supposed to be a place for tourists.

"Helen, look here," the man calls, and a mound of blue bursts from the part of the group that is farthest from us, closest to the top of the stairs.

"Oh my," says his wife. She comes down to us, her face a cloud, but recognition soon clears it up. "Well, how nice," she says. "No matter what the size of the city it's still a small world."

"You'll never believe our bumbling," the man tells me. "All that time waiting for a fellow to come along who speaks English and then we get ourselves turned around before you're two steps away."

Helen has linked one of her arms through my free one. "No time wasted, though," she assures me. "When we got off the train we found ourselves quite near the zoo. You've got some prize pandas there. Though we'd never have been able to see them if another nice gentleman hadn't let us in line."

I stand speechless while the two of them hold me captive and banter about. The maître d' is calling them to their table, so they reluctantly say good-bye. "English is the international language," Helen assures me. "You certainly have proven that."

"We've got the tower penciled in for tomorrow," says Harold. "I understand the view from there is terrific."

I stay on the stairs for a long time after they've gone, leaning hard against the wall. I have to wonder how many of the others I've wronged have finally thought that the mistake was their own. How many others, after hours of circling the city, have said to themselves, "Why hadn't I listened when that nice man was talking? Why hadn't I paid more attention?" Of course it is in the nature of some people to put the blame for things on themselves. I wanted people to wonder why a man would so purposefully point them in wrong directions, and it occurs to me now that perhaps all my deeds have missed their marks. What a depressing thought! The bar, as I leave it, is full of foreigners, each one knowing where he is and where he is going. I can hear the party of the people from Des Moines and I can hear the silly din of the celebrities, the Japanese movie stars and friends of Milo's as they herald each other's accomplishments, all talking their nonsense. All I wanted was the simple pleasure of knowing that I had wronged slightly, now, some of those who had wronged me in the past. But from now on I'll not know if it is I or themselves that they blame.

The cashier is calm-looking in her little cage near the door so I call to her, saying good night, and then I walk outside into the cold dark. Lord, lord, how many times must I get myself into these things? An old man playing his games, dredging up bits of petty bitterness. Why can't I learn to leave people alone, let them be as they will, let them be American if they must, or military or weak? Recently I have felt that I am on the cusp of a change in my life, but nothing, it would seem, moves me out of the trough I am in. It is colder now, and later than it usually is when I leave the larger bars and head back toward the Kado. People stand out in the street trying to hail taxis. Perhaps when I sleep tonight, I, like Scrooge, will be awakened by a dead friend's ghost, and tomorrow I'll be singing happily, a changed man with a wonderful change of heart. Perhaps, but I doubt it.

The Kado's sign clicks off even while I'm walking toward it, so it must be late. A breeze is pushing bits of paper at the passersby, dusting the freezing streets. When I arrive at the bar everything's dark. "Hello, Hana! Let me in,

Sachiko!" I say, rapping my knuckles lightly on the Kado's red door. Now that I'm safely away from those others I'm beginning to feel better.

"*Oi!* It is late," I call.

There is no sound from within the bar; could it be they've gone? If the customers leave early, they themselves sometimes do, but I could have sworn I saw the lights go off. "Sachiko, Sachiko," I say, but the handle's hard lock won't give much. They must have gone early. The front door is the only way out and there is no light pouring from the crack beneath it. This happens more and more often and leads me to wonder if the business is bad.

At the side of the street the wind has pushed papers up against the curb. There are taxis streaming by but they are occupied. Nevertheless I'll wait until I see the luminous handle glowing in a dark windshield, then I will raise my hand and the cab will stop for me, its automatic door opening, the driver exhibiting mechanical manners. I will go, I think, to Sachiko's room and wait for her there. But first, the problem of getting a taxi. This side street is a good place, for there are no others waiting. All the taxis that come by here are occupied, though. Certainly Sachiko could have waited, or could have closed early and come looking for me. Ah well, here's a cab so I'll ask her when I see her what the problem is. There, there, the driver sees me and is stopping. I know I will sleep during the long ride to her room. As I step from the curb his door springs open, all wide and toothless like an old man's mouth.

*

JIMMY YAMAMOTO and I had been successful in Los Angeles but were far better musicians than the others and had decided to try something different, something unique. We arrived in Japan on the edge of the decade, 1941. Our Japanese agent called himself Ike and had his whole family out to meet us. Ike was a young and jubilant man, a boy, like ourselves. Jimmy'd found him through an advertisement, and it turned out we were his sole clients. Ike had put an ad in the *American Musicians' News* only because he'd run across the application form wrapped around some peppermint candies that he'd purchased at an international bazaar. Through his desire not to be typical, Ike had apparently fallen in love with American music, a fact that was severely inhibiting his interest in family affairs. But once Ike got us he was active. He told us that there was a band for us to join, men for us to meet. "I've got jobs," he said. "An agent's worth is only in the contacts he can make."

From the very beginning, from that first day, Ike encouraged Jimmy in the courtship of his sister. His was a close family; it seemed constantly together. Yet I thought I could sense that Ike was a little at odds with them, was looking for ways to challenge the awful expectancy of tradition. His family all talked a fast kind of "real" Japanese, which was difficult for us to follow, but Ike's sister was beautiful, and Jimmy jumped at the chance to walk with her, his trumpet in a bag at his side. Ike's sister's name was Kazuko, and right away I could tell that I liked her better than Jimmy did. Ike had found us lodging near his house, and whenever Jimmy and Kazuko went for walks I did my best to go along with them. It was I who acted the part of the unwanted brother. We had only just begun to play music and there was nothing else to do.

One day, just a week after our arrival, Ike went across Tokyo in search of bookings and Jimmy and Kazuko and I went for a quiet stroll in the garden of a Buddhist temple near her house. The clouds were high and the path was empty, but before we had gone too far a calico kitten came to us, a man with a missing finger running after it. "Here, kitty," said Kazuko, for the man with the missing finger had a sack full of cats, all clamoring to get out.

The man stopped when he saw us, but soon he came up and, pointing his stub, made us imagine the missing finger and look where it led us. "That's my cat," he said. "Hand it over."

Kazuko quickly put the kitten inside her cool summer gown. "Let's go," she said, linking Jimmy's little finger with her own.

By this time I had come up close enough to hear and was smiling at the sight of a casual encounter with a fellow Buddhist there on the perfect path. "Good afternoon," I said, nodding over their shoulders at the man. "We've just arrived from America."

"I want that cat," the guy said quietly, his Japanese leaving me a little behind.

We all stood silently for a few seconds, then Jimmy took Kazuko's arm and turned her back the way we'd come. Jimmy had a certain air about him that made the man stand still. Jimmy's moustache, meager though it was, was rare in Japan for a man his age. I still hadn't sensed very well the strangeness of the situation and stayed facing the fellow until Jimmy and Kazuko had walked away.

"You think I can't get through you, you little shit," the guy said, walking right up to me.

"What?"

I could understand what the man was saying all right, but I had no idea what it meant. Had Kazuko really stolen his cat?

"Maybe I didn't make myself clear," he said, then he leaned against me and slowly stuck a knife a half-inch or so into my abdomen.

The guy took his time taking the knife away, and while

he waited I stood on tiptoes and felt the blade slide sideways. "See you later," he finally said, laughing and letting me down. "You can keep the cat."

When he left I turned to look for my two friends, then slowly sat down. There was moisture all about my middle, and it took a minute, after I began to yell, for Jimmy to hear me and hurry back to help. Kazuko cried when she saw my wound and the kitten laid its head on the edge of her obi to see what was going on. "Japan is not this way!" Kazuko said.

"Christ, man," said Jimmy. "You can still play, can't you? Where are you hurt?"

"My stomach," I said. "Why did you take the man's cat?"

Kazuko knelt by my side and whispered. "He was a member of the *yakuza* class, a criminal. He would have fattened the cat up just to skin it and sell its hide for the making of a *shamisen*."

"Can you walk?" Jimmy asked. "Can you stand?" While I sat on the path I kept my hands cupped about my wound, afraid to pull my shirt up to see what damage was actually done. Though the blood was warm at the center of the wound it was cold about its edges.

"I don't want anything coming out," I told them. "If I stand up something might slip."

Jimmy began unbuttoning my shirt from the bottom, his unpracticed hands shaking. Kazuko cried and paced in a small circle around us and finally said, "I will go to the temple building. The priests there will know what to do."

She started to hurry off, but came back quickly and crouched beside me, the kitten, calm and curious, sitting in the center of her two hands.

"Here," she said. "You've got to keep it. You've saved its life."

She sat the calico cat on the curve of my knee then set

out again toward the Buddhist building at the center of the temple grounds. The cat could smell the blood and was interested enough to stay where she had put it.

"It's not too bad," Jimmy said, peering inside my parted shirt. "It's crooked, shaped like an *l*, I think, though there is too much blood to be sure. There's a little line coming up from the outside which might make it look more like a *u*."

I grimaced as he chatted on, more demonstrative than ever before, interested in my wound, in the line the blade made, the design of it. I could see Kazuko running, cutting across the paths, her clothes bunched in her hands and held high enough to allow for longer steps. She ran around a pond, then slowed as she ascended the steep steps and disappeared into the dark mouth of the building.

There was a lot of blood on my clothes. Jimmy jumped up and then sat back down again. "Do you feel all right?" he wanted to know. "You're not going to faint or anything, are you?"

I held my stomach, laughing a little, then motioned for him to take the cat. In all the time I'd known him this was the first time I'd had his full attention. Before he'd always been vague, a daydreamer, never really paying attention to the things I said. Jimmy and I were matched well musically, but after we got off the stage he was an enigma to me. He didn't like to do anything, had no friends, never practiced his horn. He was quiet and careful with his words, but he wasn't well educated and I had trouble discovering things we could do that would interest him. It was only when we worked that I could see the sparkle in his eyes. When we worked he held his horn high and played hard. He knew every song there was, and he was quick to take pleasure in the playing of others.

Two pale priests arrived with Kazuko. They had a thick

futon and unrolled it beside me. "Get on," said one of the priests. "Sit over here."

I shifted my weight a little but couldn't move. I rolled onto my back, my knees still bunched, then let them lift me up and place me on the pallet. "It's soft," I said.

Jimmy tucked the calico cat under my arm and they each took a corner, lifting me lightly up off the ground. Kazuko kept her eyes down but carried me as well as any of the others. "Ouch," I said; "can't you be more careful?" We were working our way back toward the temple, and though the four of them stepped carefully, each jar, each path stone slipping silently out from under a foot, caused me pain.

Kazuko cried when I spoke and with each cry my heart went out to her. She was lovelier than any of the girls I had known at home. I had learned that she liked to practice the tea ceremony and when, a few days before, she had introduced me to her old teacher, I had been proud. A slight bit of perspiration welled up on the outskirts of her perfect nose, and sick as I was, I wanted to reach up and wipe it off. "Kazuko Maki," I thought to myself, and felt another searing pain as one of the priests put his foot down too hard and the *futon* fell.

"Jesus Christ!" said Jimmy, glancing at Kazuko, whose corner it was that had come down first. She was horrified, so though the pain was bad I held my tongue, somehow not crying out. "Fine," I said. "Nothing to worry about."

They picked me up again and in a moment I was waiting on the steps of the temple while the priests prepared a room for me. One of them brought out a bottle of iodine and poured it about my belly, first pulling the shirt painfully away from the places where it stuck to the drying wound. This time I couldn't help crying. "Holy Mother!" I said. "Ahhh!" The medicine hurt more than the original stabbing, and when I shouted, using language that my schoolmates had used, the cat came up meowing, eyeing the stain suspiciously and smelling it as it spread across my shirt.

When they finally carried me inside the temple the air was cool under the big Buddha image that dominated the room. We passed through the great main hall and along a wooden walkway to the small rooms where the priests stayed, where they learned their lessons, where the master struck at them with a large stick or clapped loudly when they were slow-witted or wrong.

The rooms we passed were small, like cells, with no windows or doors. In some of them young priests prayed, or sat sleeping. My arrival, the noise of the four of them carrying me past, had caused some curiosity, and in a moment the monks and their master all appeared. The master had been told of my arrival and had sent the iodine out to me. He searched now for its stain, for proof that the priests had carried out his orders.

The master turned to me. "Was there any cause or was the attack unprovoked? I'll need to know, for the police are coming and if you tell me I will keep them away from you."

"We were arguing over a cat," I said.

Some of the priests laughed but the master motioned with his hands so they stopped. The cat was curled up beside me, out of sight. Jimmy and Kazuko had joined hands so my pain was increased.

"A calico cat," said Kazuko.

The master spoke softly and the monks carried me into one of their small rooms to rest. Someone said the police were waiting, so I finally mentioned what was on my mind. "Has anyone called for a doctor?" I asked.

When I was in the room alone the cat came out, its three colors not very impressive in the dim light. Kazuko had lingered a little so I let the cat lick me, but as soon as she was gone I pushed it away. Dogs had been a part of my past, but never cats.

30

After that I must have dozed, for when next I became aware of my surroundings there was a doctor kneeling by me, a needle stuck in my side. The doctor grunted as American doctors do, and when I asked him what he thought he laughed and said my friend had been wrong. My cut was not *l*-shaped, nor was it a *u*. "It is a little circle," he said. "An *o* if we must gauge our wounds by the western alphabet. No serious damage done. If his knife had been sharper he'd have severed your abdominal wall, but as it is, it's just tissue, a little island of fat separated from the pudgy continent that is yourself."

When the doctor left, Kazuko and Jimmy sneaked out again too, leaving, for once, some distance between their hands. "Come get your cat," I called but Kazuko did not return, so the cat remained, calm in the corner. I slept and woke and slept. When it got dark the monks began to moan. The one in whose room I stayed crawled in and took up so little space in the corner that I could barely see him.

"Sorry for the intrusion," I said. "I would gladly go home now if you'd show me the way."

The monk sat staring but he would not speak. Indeed, all day it was only the master who had spoken.

"My cat is hungry," I said. "Is there milk? Something for it to eat?"

"We are vegetarians," he said.

"Is there a vegetable then, that it could eat? I wouldn't ask for myself."

The monk studied me, then stood and sat again in the doorway where he would be seen by someone passing. "The master may not like it," he said.

I must have slept for several hours during the day, for now, at dusk, I was wide awake. My wound was still aching but since I knew my stomach would not slip I was inclined to get out of that solitary cell. The master came out of the shadows quietly and laid a bamboo rod on the nimble monk's shoulders.

"Why do you sit in the doorway?" he asked.

"The cat is hungry. Our guest says so."

The master motioned to the monk and they both went off, and in a moment the master was back by himself with a little bowl of milk and a large sack of oranges.

"Do you like Zen parables?" he asked me, putting the oranges between us and peeling two.

"I don't know any," I said. "I'm from the United States. I've only been in Japan a week."

"Once the monk Nansen saw the monks of the eastern and western halls fighting over a cat. He seized the cat and told the monks, 'If any of you says a good word you can save the cat.' No one answered so Nansen cut the cat in two. That evening Joshi returned and Nansen told him what had happened that day. Joshi removed his sandals and placed them upon his head. Nansen said, 'If you had been there you could have saved the cat.' "

I looked at the master but there was so little light in the room that I could not see his face. My cat, unconcerned, kept lapping up the milk in the corner.

"You get it?" asked the master.

"Don't fight over cats? Let them live as they will?"

"In this case it is true that the cat would have made a fine *shamisen*. Listen."

Magically the master pulled a *shamisen* from beneath his robes. He was a large man and when he put the instrument against his middle I could not see it. He began to play. My father on his farm had played a *shamisen*, but its strains had never been like this. Where my father's music had been slow and stumbling, the master's was smooth and wonderful. All the monks around us in their cells were listening, I could tell. I assumed he'd play for just a moment, so that I could hear all the uses the hide of a cat could be put to, but he continued, without stopping, for half an hour. He played the tunes my father could play and the ones he just listened to as well. And indeed, even the cat, when it finished its milk, wandered closer, put its head across my foot and began to purr.

As the master played I began to fear that he might also have a sword or a knife stuck somewhere under his robes and when he finished he'd pull it out and cut the cat. But when he did stop the cat crawled up on his lap and he merely put his heavy hands around it and began to stroke.

"Your playing is so beautiful," I said. "Though I have never lived in Japan it made me feel at home."

"My playing is part of it, but the calico cat that sleeps across the center of the instrument is part of it as well. This *shamisen* itself once purred in my hands, once caught mice under the Buddha and lapped up the milk the monks gave it. Its hide is so wondrous that it can contain a cat of any size. It will stretch. It could accommodate an even larger *shamisen*."

"Why not just leave it alone?" I said, hearing a certain whining in my voice.

"Do not fool yourself into thinking that the cat cares. Life and death are one to it."

The master waved his hands above him and laughed, somehow ending the discussion. I picked up the cat and tried to look at it in the dark. "If this cat were yours would you kill it?" I asked. "Would you fatten it up and then steal its skin so that you could have another *shamisen* as fine as the one you played tonight?"

"Certainly not," said the priest.

"You see. Once the cat got close to you you'd give it a name and there would be no more talk of killing."

"No," he said. "It would simply be silly to have two *shamisen*. And if the cat were mine I'd be very surprised. This *shamisen* is mine but the cat could not be."

I sighed and decided to stop. What kind of repartee could I accomplish with this man?

"Forget the cat," I said. "It is people we are supposed to care about."

"Come what may," said the priest.

I was thinking suddenly about Kazuko and Jimmy again and was surprised when the priest said, "Of course the secret of receiving is in not wanting."

I sat there again, smiling a little. This man made his living saying things like that to all the new monks of the temple.

"You've been very kind in caring for my wound. Do you think the doctor would mind if I went home now?"

"He would not mind," said the master.

I stood, knowing after only a few hours that I could not lead a life like this. The master moved a bit to the side and stood in one motion. I was surprised by how short he was. "Take your cat," he said. "It could come in handy." He laughed a little and so did I.

The master motioned to the others as we walked back through the building, so they all fell in behind. The Buddha was brighter than I expected it would be at night, and I worried that maybe that man was still out there somewhere, waiting to wedge his knife into me once more.

"The moon is up," said the master.

The little cat was tucked inside my shirt, sleeping around the soft edges of my wound. I decided to say one thing more to the master.

"I don't *not* care for the cat. You don't think that, do you?"

This time I made him laugh hard so the other monks laughed too. For a moment they held their laughter in, then it burst, echoing a little way over the fragile garden, over the low trees.

"Good night," called the master as I started down the steps.

I didn't like their laughing, so without saying anything I started to walk away. The moon was everywhere and I forgot my fear. The night air was invigorating. It was cool. Even the cat must have felt it, for within my shirt it began to stir. It stretched a little and pushed its head between the buttons. It wasn't a bad cat, its eyes wide, its whiskers white. When the monks stopped laughing the cat seemed startled. When I stepped onto the main street it was inside my shirt again, but its claws were wide now, and pushing a little into the flesh around my wound.

*

WHEN I think about those early days of my arrival, those weeks when war was folding around the world, the vision that I have of myself is as my son is now. The thoughts that found me then were fatuous at best, yet passionate and strong were my emotions. When an old man views the young in himself, there is much he can find to disdain, much that will make him laugh, more that will make him cringe.

My son is all Japanese, his language, his habits, his ways. Yet I must not be too hard on him for acting whimsically, for the poor quality of his music, or the ease with which he is distracted. When he was little I'd look at him and see the traces of another man's face in his small one, but I loved him just the same. His mother would hold him out to me and I would take him and feel all the lighter for it.

When my son made his first recording I gave him little help, but he was able to release it because of me nevertheless. The record jacket was gold with a picture of Milo standing at the seaside with the wind all rough in his hair.

He was holding in his hands another record, and, of course, it was one of mine, my first, and if you looked carefully you could see, in turn, a small likeness of myself at the same sea. Until the time of my son's record, modern music in Japan had been poor. With it, however, a downward spiral was started, the bottom of which is still not visible. And now my son's music is no longer the worst that can be found here. I, in my way, have tried to make him feel better by making my television show his music's equal, but the efforts seem lost on him. He and I have both become popular for the damage that we do, though I, of course, am trying, and my son, I'm afraid, is not.

When Milo was little, when he was six, he fell a story from the school window and I can remember waiting for his recovery. The war had been over a while but I still was not ready, not nearly ready, to renew the awful agony of feeling. I can remember my wife saying that from six-year-olds the world should withhold its anger, yet that Milo would roll from the window made me mad at Milo and as soon as he was well enough I slapped him. And that simple slap, so unforgivable, has stayed between us all these years. Its echo, sometimes, sends dull sensations through my fingers when I see my son.

By the time Milo recovered from his fall I had already begun my rise from the ranks of out-of-work entertainers. I was on my own after the war but by then the nation's interest in English had been born. And jazz seemed central to the underpinnings of the new society, as if by adopting it the Japanese could prove to the occupiers that they too were truly human. I was held up as an example of a good Japanese because I could sing so nicely in English, I could sing so accent-free. And yet, by the Americans I was held in contempt. A short while after my songs began to circulate, a little while after a large segment of my society began making furious forays into the world of late-night dancing, I, along with others of my kind, was called to a perfunctory hearing. We stood before American officers while a staff artist drew a depiction of our poor postures, our unrepentant attitudes.

"Teddy Maki of Los Angeles," the court clerk called, so I stepped forward.

A colonel spoke softly, asking me, "Did you, Mr. Maki, fight for the Japanese during the recent war?"

"No, sir."

"You did not?"

"I didn't fight, sir."

"Did you wear the Japanese army uniform? Did you eat with the Japanese soldiers? Did you speak Japanese with them and share their jokes?"

"I had no choice."

"Then the answer is yes."

"Yes."

"Are you aware that taking up arms against the forces of the United States is grounds for imprisonment? Grounds for loss of citizenship?"

"I have recently been told so."

"You are a popular singer, are you not, Mr. Maki? Do you think it is right that you should go free after having turned against your country so?"

"I haven't done anything wrong," I said. "I've turned against no one. Circumstances caused me to do what I did. Any other course would have cost me my life."

I had said, already, more than I wanted to, more than I'd told myself I would when I arrived. Most of my acquaintances were dead. Who would care what happened to me?

The colonel looked back and forth, his face all haughty from my listlessness, my lack of remorse.

"What would your family think, Mr. Maki, if they knew what you'd done?"

From what I could gather my father had lost his land and my uncle his grocery store a few months before they'd enlisted. My mother and brothers and younger cousins waited for them in a makeshift prison, somewhere in the desert, east of where the farm had been.

"They are all scattered," I said. "Victims of the war."

The colonel seemed to tire of me but cleared his throat and asked, "Are you a communist, Mr. Maki? Have you ever been?"

"I am not a communist. I don't care," I said.

The colonel stood and stretched his legs but let me stay standing before him. Finally he asked, "Do you swear that everything you have said is true?"

"Do you mean today?" I asked him.

He was irritated by my insolence but there were many others waiting so he let me go, keeping with him my American citizenship, invisible though it was. When I turned toward the small and silent audience the first face I saw was Milo's, and he was smiling.

"You did well, Daddy," he said, as we were leaving by the back door. He held by its broken strings a toy guitar I'd given him and trailed it slowly along the lockers that lined the hall.

*

JIMMY and Kazuko were married and I was best man. Jimmy and I had never talked about my feelings for the woman he would wed but he knew, and I kept thinking I saw a soft smile of satisfaction crossing his lips. They were married at the end of November, 1941, when the mood in the city was one of caution. Crowds stood in front of public billboards where the daily newspapers were pinned up, and though my reading was slow, I could read the characters for America in the headlines, and knew there were embargoes. I saw the steaming face of Admiral Yamamoto, and read the word *war*.

Jimmy and Kazuko stood in the same Buddhist temple where I'd received my wound. There were others waiting; it was a day of weddings. As soon as the ceremony was done we left by the side door and walked through the garden just as we had on the day of the cat. All of Kazuko's family was there; her tea ceremony teacher was the only other outside guest. The weather was cold and the sky was high and clear. People smiled at us, mothers pointing out the formal kimono, one child crying when she saw the powder-white face of the bride.

On the day of Pearl Harbor, on that Sunday when the sailors and civilians of Hawaii were turning their heads skyward, it was Monday in Tokyo and I was on my way to the public bath. Since the wedding the week before, I'd been living alone, though the building which housed me held hundreds of students, boys from the countryside, up to Tokyo for an education. Jimmy and Kazuko had taken the back room of her mother's house. It was a small room, but big enough for them to unfold their *futon* and lie together, big enough for them to fold into each other in my imagination and make me miserable.

The public bath was three city blocks away by Los Angeles standards, though the road that got me there was small and snakelike, winding near the rice merchant's, past a few neighborhood restaurants and bars. I was taking the walk calmly, keeping the married Kazuko out of my mind, when I noticed that the streets were more active than usual, that even some of the students from where I lived were lounging about, their uniform collars askew and their hats tipped back.

"Hey!" one of them called when he saw me. "What do you think?"

"I'm headed for the bath," I said. "What? No school today?"

The student and two of his friends came over and stood on the street with me, their faces bright. I had rarely seen them at the dormitory, but they knew I was from America.

"He doesn't know," the student said. "How could he not know?"

They all shook their heads. "We are at war with America!" they said. "We are all going into the army. We are finished with school forever!"

With Jimmy's wedding on my mind I hadn't thought of politics in a while. I knew there was tension between the two countries, but war was ridiculous. The United States was so much bigger, so much stronger.

"War?" I asked. "Who told you? You're joking."

"You have been to the United States," one of them said. "You speak English. You could be our spy."

"Yes," said another. "You must go to that country and tell us what they say. There aren't many people who can speak both languages."

The students laughed at the prospect, but then got caught up in the logistics of it and while they were working it out I slipped away.

My God, war. I'd been getting some mail from home; Uncle had written that my mother and father were having trouble on the farm, were in need of their son's help, but no one had ever mentioned war. What would happen to all of them? I had to get home. I turned off the street that led to the bath and headed for Kazuko's. I would leave tomorrow, but what would Jimmy do now that he was married? There were so many unanswered questions. War was something we had with the Germans, not with the Japanese. War was to be fought against a country's enemies, not against its friends, and America and Japan had always been friends. Surely the students must have been mistaken. It was a tease.

Something to keep me from asking why they weren't in school.

I hurried along the street and saw everyone now as hurrying too. It was no joke. I stopped at the bulletin board by the farmer's bank, then ran past it once I'd recognized the word for war once again. Now it was easy to read for it was written thickly, not in the paper's usual print, but by hand, its bold brush strokes sending chills through me, its very size making me admit that it was probably true, there was war between the United States and Japan.

My cat had been staying at Kazuko's house since the wedding. I'd told them that it was a gift but they'd said that if cats cannot be owned then they cannot be given. When I entered their garden I saw the cat standing coolly at the base of the old fig tree that they had. I could hear other voices so I knocked lightly then coughed once and Kazuko slid back the door.

"Oh, what will we do?" she said, taking my arm and pulling me inside. "Jimmy is so upset. What will we do? What will happen to all of us?"

Even during a crisis you'd think she'd know better than to stand so close. The look of her there in front of me, her naked hand holding mine. I was coming undone so I quickly said, "We're going to be spies, Jimmy and I. We're going to be double agents."

From the living room I could hear the sound of sobs so I quieted, removing my shoes, and stood as tall as I could beside Kazuko on the tan tatami. Inside the room there were teacups everywhere, half empty and strewn about. Kazuko's mother was crying, her grandfather was remembering the Russian war with photographs placed on the tables and taped around the walls, and Ike was smiling.

When Kazuko's mother saw me she stepped into the kitchen for a clean cup. Jimmy was sitting silently in the corner.

"Tell me, Teddy," the grandfather said, "don't you think

we can win? Jimmy has just said that he does not and I'm out to prove him wrong."

I took the tea and sat on a *zabuton* near the central table. "America is one hundred times bigger than Japan," I told him, "one hundred times as strong."

"But we've beaten America already. Admiral Yamamoto is not young but he is smart. He went to Harvard College and knows the American mind better than the two of you. Admiral Yamamoto says we can win."

The old man began pushing photos of the Russian war into my hands. In one there was a slight young man, standing sober-looking against the side of a captured wagon. "That's me," he said. "I fought in that war. We were stationed in Korea. We won against all odds that time too."

The old man kept talking, but his gaze returned to the pictures, so I took the opportunity to speak to Jimmy.

"What do you think, my man?" I asked. "We're in for it now, wouldn't you say?" I tried to grin, tried to stay cheerful, for Kazuko was still near me, her hand still inches from my own.

Jimmy looked at me and then past me at his wife. The calico cat had come in and was walking figure-eights around the grandfather's legs. I spoke again, a little more urgently, this time whispering. "What will we do?" I poked Jimmy hard on the shoulder and he sighed as if deflated.

"We're stuck, that's all," he said. "Especially me. Most of the official Americans are gone already. There is nothing we can do."

Ike was next to us, smiling enigmatically, still cheerful and calm. "Don't take it so hard," he said. "They'll issue us fine clothes and train us in karate. When we get out we'll be able to defend ourselves. No more worries about *yakuza* in the park."

Kazuko's grandfather, sensing his loss of control, came over to us and dropped another bundle of photographs in our laps. "Ike's right," he said. "War is terrible but it is romantic. When you boys get your uniforms you'll feel better than you do now. You'll see. You'll walk tall, step crisply. There is no greater honor than to die in battle for your country."

"Christ," said Jimmy.

"Most of my comrades died in the war," the grandfather assured us. "Those of us who survived have had to live with that knowledge. It is much better to die than to have to explain why you are still alive."

Jimmy and I kept quiet while the old man talked, and, oddly, the others in the room seemed to calm under his words. Ike nodded like a confidant. Kazuko still sat next to me, but the tension in her body was going, a patriotic persuasion taking her. Finally she said, "That's what you'll have to do. Enlist. You are Japanese before you are Americans. Enlist and fight!"

"We're musicians!" I said, sitting up straight and raising my voice. "We came here to play music. How about it, Ike? You're our manager. You should be helping us get back home."

Ike seemed worried by my tone. "Manager maybe," he said, "but not magician. What can I do?"

I guess I had been shouting, for Kazuko looked at me oddly then slid across the tatami toward Jimmy. She took his arm. "You can't go back," she told him. "You are my husband. You are Japanese and must do your duty."

Even in the heat of the moment I felt the sting of her movement away from me. They had only been married a week. Not enough time for me to mend. Kazuko was breaking my heart but I sighed and said what I had to say. "We may look Japanese but we're Americans! We speak English! This is too much to ask of anyone. There is a war starting!"

Everyone in the room, even the grandfather, stopped what they were doing and looked at me. The morning newspaper was face-up on the floor, the characters for war still spilling across its front. Kazuko's mother went to the garden and looked about to see if any of the neighbors had heard me, but the street was empty. "Watch your tongue, Teddy," she said, coming back. "We mustn't say things we do not mean. We will be misunderstood."

The grandfather's face was quizzical. He alternately peered at me and threw his eyes toward the ceiling in a gesture of futility.

"All right," I said. "I'm sorry. This is Japan, but I'm not bloody well enlisting."

"Quiet, Teddy," said Ike, and Kazuko put her fingers to her lips, her other hand gently upon my forearm. "Shh," she said. "Silence is what is called for now. It is time for us to show our strength."

Jimmy just sat there silently, not adding his voice to mine, a model for Kazuko's admiration. I think he knew if he said anything he'd give himself away, for all of us were looking at him. They all thought him so strong, but I suspected that the prospect of violent war had wrenched the voice from his throat.

"Say something, Jimmy," I said. "Will you enlist? Will you bear arms against the Americans?"

When I spoke to him this time I spoke in English so the others kept quiet. But when Jimmy finally answered it was in Japanese again.

"I think I will enlist," he said. "It is the only thing to do."

While Jimmy had been quiet the reality of the war seemed to wait at the edges of the room, but when he broke his silence it all came in on us. The grandfather dug into his box of war relics and, pulling out an old battle flag, draped it across Jimmy's shoulders, the red rays of the flag falling down his arms. The patriotism shared by Kazuko and her mother and grandfather immediately centered on the flag, on the strength that came from that streaming sun. Even Ike seemed to bask in its warmth.

"You're all nuts," I said, but the fight had gone out of my voice.

"Most young men our age are gone already," Ike said softly, his eyes still fixed on the flag. "I'm still here because I'm helping to organize the ward." He shook himself loose a little and said, "Don't worry, it will be great. I think I can guarantee that we'll all stay together."

While Jimmy was statued in the center of the room and Ike was still talking, while that battle flag still streamed from my friend so electrically, there was nothing I could do. I still hoped, though, that if I got him alone we could think of some way to get home. I walked out of the room and into the garden, the little cat following me. "Well," I said to it, "you'll be safe. All of the *shamisen* makers will be at war." But it would not look at me. Over the past months I had taken to running my fingers along the edges of my knife wound whenever I saw the cat. Until now it had been a point of some pride with me, a wound taken voluntarily and for love.

"All right," said Jimmy, standing beside me, the flag finally gone, "What would you have me do?" He spoke English, but softly. Since we were outside we wanted to keep our eyes open for the neighbors.

"Christ, Jimmy!" I said. "This is no joke. We're in Japan and Japan is at war with our country! What will we do? How will we get out of here?"

He smiled that distant smile of his. "Resign yourself to it," he said. "I've been up all morning thinking about it and there is nothing we can do. It is better to come to that realization now than later. I'm talking about staying alive, Teddy. If anyone thinks our ambition is to join the Americans we'll be killed."

"Jimmy," I said, "we've got to get home."

"Don't be optimistic," he said. "Be careful. Don't mess it up."

The cat crawled halfway up the fig tree and meowed, waiting for me to rescue it. Jimmy was looking straight at me, his hands somehow strong again at his sides. He picked up the cat and handed it to me. "Enlist," he said. "Come with me and enlist today. Don't mention America. With luck we might make the military band. With luck you might grow old in Los Angeles, Teddy, just as you've always hoped you would."

The grandfather came and motioned us in for tea and rice cakes, the beginning ritual for our long days ahead. Kazuko was wearing a more beautiful and formal kimono, and her mother had turned the flowers in the tokonoma in fresh directions. Only Ike, still playful, had maintained himself. He had slipped into his grandfather's old uniform and was turning about the room like a fashion model.

When Jimmy stepped inside, the cat leaped from my arms and followed him, leaving me alone in the garden once more. I could see the Japanese battle flag, vaguely, through the open doors. The grandfather was holding it up, trying to make it flutter in the breezeless room.

During the next days things happened fast. Kazuko calmed, finally, to my initial fears, and the rest of the family accepted me again. The newspapers and radios told people what to do, where men should report, and which factories were in need of female laborers. The community was mobilized. Kazuko and her mother began working making uniforms. Ike was gone from the house most of the time, coming in and out like a man with a purpose. He seemed to have warmed to his new role, making the change from band manager to military man with ease. Then one night he came back with ward instructions. "Of course all the club dates are canceled" was all he ever said about the band.

The athletic field next to the local middle school was to be used for induction ceremonies, and Ike, now clearly in charge, said he'd get us proper clothes, tell us the times, bring us first news of any battles that might have started, of Japanese victories at sea.

Jimmy liked to remain within the confines of his house, but I found it hard to stay off the streets. Students like the ones I lived with were in evidence everywhere. Flags appeared, like the one the grandfather had, and businesses were booming. I rode one day, on a bus, down around the Imperial Palace. I imagined the Emperor sitting somewhere inside, his aides all about him, maps of the United States staring down at him from his wall. What would happen? I wondered. How long could such a war last?

The people around me were full of goodwill toward each other, and nobody was uninvolved. Barbers about town were busy shaving heads. Trucks with loudspeakers roamed here and there, giving information to the general public that the family and I had gotten from Ike the day or the night before. By the beginning of the new year the Japanese had beaten the British at Singapore and the Americans in Manila. "Asia stands united," our loudspeakers told us, "and will stay that way. From this day forward the western world will have to pay for the pleasures that it takes, for the natural and human resources that it has, until now, taken from us at will."

Ike's grandfather was with Jimmy in the garden and had shaved half his head by the time I walked in one evening. "Good," he said, "you're next." The ward had received its orders.

Kazuko came out with a large framed photograph of Ike in her hands. She held a camera. "We're going to make an altar," she said cheerfully. "Ike and Jimmy, and your photo too, Teddy. We'll have a shrine to the sacrifices you all are making."

Jimmy was sitting silently again, very serious, so I said nothing. What was the use? When he finished with Jimmy the old man motioned to me, so I sat down in his chair, my feet among Jimmy's black droppings, and watched as Kazuko positioned her husband in a solemn pose, his American-made clothes still clinging to him. Jimmy's cheekbones were high and he looked smaller without his hair. The camera she used was one we'd brought from the United States, and as she clicked away with it I could feel my own hair joining Jimmy's. Here the war had upset every household; I wondered what was happening in America.

That same evening, after we lost our hair, Ike came to the house and we left for the middle school playground and the beginnings of the real war. Kazuko and her mother and grandfather walked with us, talking, taking turns telling us how glorious it would be, how the radio said the American fleet was already beaten and that the rest of the war would be merely a mop-up, a claiming of lands, an administration. Pictures of Pearl Harbor were posted everywhere, and it did look bad. Could it be true? Could Japan really be in charge? Could they be winning?

At the edge of the playground the families of all the soldiers fused together, swaying as a single body, kimono colors blending. The officer in charge, a man named Nakamura, shouted through a megaphone, over the straight faces of the new recruits, and as he spoke silence settled in. *Glory* was one word I recognized. The honor to die in battle does not come to every generation. The Bushido spirit, between conflicts, is a sleeping tiger, but is born of us on this playground here today. Stand straight, young men, and remember the word *victory*. Some of you will die, but the rest must go on, not even taking time to regret that your lives still linger within you. The code of the Bushido cannot wither, only our flimsy flesh can do that, so do not worry.

On and on the officer spoke. He was the commander of

the unit to which we all would be attached, and he liked what he saw. Jimmy stood as straight as those next to us, so I tried standing straight too. I was afraid. I could no longer see Kazuko in the crowd around us. The poor and private streets of east Los Angeles came to mind and for just a second I began to cry.

"The wooden soldiers of the rice nation will be sorry to have challenged us," said the officer, "for we are a people who know the beauty and special glory of violent death! Throughout our long history we have fought according to our code, and we have never been defeated! We are Japan! There is no other nation that, in any way, resembles ours. We are Japanese! In this war we will be victorious for there is no other possible outcome!"

The crowd came together spontaneously, the soldiers and the spectators too.

"Banzai!" they shouted.

"Remember that our cause is an honorable one!"

"Banzai!"

"Remember Pearl Harbor and the glorious start it has given us!"

"Banzai!"

"Remember the Bushido and your Japanese ancestors!"

"Banzai! Banzai! Banzai!"

Everyone in the crowd raised their hands, fingers toward the clouds, shouting. Around the outskirts I could see the swaying civilians stretching skyward too. "Banzai!" Ike joined the chant and so did Jimmy and I. The air was electric, the urge to fight in them all. Once, quickly, I thought I saw Kazuko, her face tense, tears streaming. My skin was tight, raising itself into gooseflesh. I had the urge to speak in English, so I turned to Jimmy but held my tongue. I felt that to say something in English just then might mean my life, for English orders reality so differently that the whole spectacle might seem silly and I would laugh. When the speech was over we all stayed standing, waiting as men walked among us with instructions. The three of us kept calm, not saying anything to each other. There were buses parked along the far street, away from where Kazuko was, and as we walked toward them Jimmy didn't once look back, yet my head was constantly turned. As we boarded our bus I stuck my face up near Jimmy's ear and whispered. "Banzai," I told him. "Remember your Japanese ancestors." I kept craning my neck for Kazuko but the crowd was immense. Jimmy just sat there, not next to me but up next to his brother-in-law, in the seat ahead. The buses began to move before I was ready for them. They went in a direction I did not know, out into the endless city. Our comrades were quiet, their hairless heads dimly shining. There was a corporal in the front who kept talking to us. We were going to train in some place I'd never heard of. We were heading for parts of Japan where neither Jimmy nor I had ever been.

*

LONG after Jimmy and Ike and I finished our training, long after we'd been assigned to a unit and left Japan, I got a letter from Harry, my father, his last. The letter came through Kazuko, tucked deep within one she'd written to Jimmy, and the danger of it was that it was written in English. We were in the Philippines and there were American prisoners everywhere. We were members of a backup unit, and our job was to set up local administrations, to keep the people under control, to let them know that the rules were to be obeyed and that we'd come down swiftly upon the heads of violators.

Amazingly, Ike had been true to his word. He had kept us together throughout it all. Ike was a sergeant, and whenever he had to take someone on a small neighborhood patrol with him he chose the two of us. In certain sections of these little towns, we'd worry about snipers. The Japanese weren't very popular with the Filipinos. The Americans had been occupiers too, but apparently of a variety less rigid, less repulsive to the native population. There were very many bands of mountain guerrillas, and though the invasion was over, though the Japanese victory was secure, many of our men had been killed and we weren't taking any chances.

It was on one of these patrols, on one of the dark mud streets, that Jimmy took the letter out and gave it to me. We almost never spoke English, but when he handed it to me he said, "This came. Kazuko took a great chance getting it to you."

The envelope was creased and bent but it was mail, and it was from home. Father had written the address in Japanese and, who knows how, had found some way to post it. As near as I can remember, it was February when Jimmy gave me the letter.

I stepped into a poorly lit shack, a little store where townspeople could buy bits of things, ingredients for the making of a meal, a notebook, a little candy. The woman who ran the store was silent when she saw me. She kept her back against the wall, her eyes on my uniform, on the big gun that I carried. I sat at a square table and she immediately brought me tea. This is what the letter said:

My dear Teddy:
    This is an exercise to make me stop thinking of you because I know the letter can't find you wherever you are. Are you surprised to hear from your old man? Not so old though, cause I'll be leaving in the morning for Europe. You should see me all dressed to kill like I used to do when I was young. Even farmers can fight, says your mother, even grocers, say your cousins and your uncle's wife. The ironical world is folding in upon us, isn't it, Teddy? You

remember how you used to help on the farm? No problem no longer though for the farm is gone. Your uncle's store too, such a popular hangout for you and that Jimmy, has got boards nailed around its windows and the sign is down. Things have been hard here but I bet they are harder there, for you. Your mother has thought out loud that you are dead. What a joke, right? She saved all the little parts of you she could find when we left the farm and she made a little altar out of them. I feel you are fine but I let her keep the altar anyway. Your mother will be staying here (we are living not too far from the farm now with all the other Japanese they could round up) while I and your uncle and many of the other men go fight. The army won't let us fight in the Pacific, but that's ok because we don't want to anyway, most of us.

Nobody could have been more surprised than me when the Japanese bombed Pearl Harbor. Things must have changed a lot since I lived there, that's all I've got to say. The United States and Japan have always been friends and though the friendship between them hasn't exactly been 50–50, I sure never thought it would end in war. Everyone here is upset about it. That is why we are living all together like this, they think maybe there are spies among us. Still, life is not as nice as it used to be, not at all. I keep thinking of planting, of all my good ground gone to waste. Even the small farms could help supply food to our fighting boys, I told them, but the answer was no. Things are bad, Teddy boy. In order to illustrate this point I'll tell you about a poster they've got. It is called, "How to tell a Jap from a Chinese," and it's pretty funny really. There are these two guys standing side by side and one of them has got good posture and the other bad. One of them has fine teeth and a big smile where the other is sneering out at the photographer like a mad dog. One is tall and one is short; one handsome, one ugly. And there are little notes on the poster, arrows pointing to parts of the body so that the public will not make the mistake of thinking one is one when he is the other. I don't know, they both look Japanese to me. We've got some pretty ugly guys, but a few handsome ones as well.

Do you know why I'm writing in English? It is because I don't want your mother reading over my shoulder. She is so nervous lately. If she thought I was writing to you she'd go to her altar and there'd be no peace tonight. I wonder if they have you in jail over there for being an American? Whatever they're doing, it won't go on forever, and when the war is over your countrymen will be there to set things straight, remember that.

Well, Teddy, God bless you. I just thought that this is the first letter I've ever written in English. Not bad, huh? Say hello to Jimmy for all of us. Even your mother. When the war is over and we get together again we'll all laugh about all the funny things that happened. Do you think so? When we get to Europe we're gonna fight like hell.

Sincerely yours,
Daddy (Harry Maki)

The woman who owned the store was watching me carefully and as soon as I finished my tea she brought me more. When I stood to pay for it she waved me away. Jimmy and Ike were just outside the door.

"Did you tear it up?" Jimmy asked.

When I'd finished the letter I'd been surprised to think that my father had never meant much to me. It was always my uncle whom I'd looked up to, my uncle, the city man. But I didn't want to tear up the letter. I asked Jimmy if he wanted to read it, but when he declined I kept it tucked inside my shirt.

"They're fighting in Europe," I told him. "They could all be dead by now."

*

REALLY, the length of World War II was deceiving. It began very quickly but ended in a casual way, and many times. Historians might say that after the battle of Midway the war lost any of the suspense it had, but though the Japanese were defeated they held on everywhere, dug in, kept the propaganda of virtual victory alive in the hearts of the citizens at home. And in 1942 all was still undecided. The prisoners we held were skinny, in some cases, emaciated. Jimmy and I began to be known for our English-speaking ability. With Ike telling us what to do, we began, very occasionally, to interrogate, to ask the captives to tell us what they knew of the movements of their troops.

There were night patrols constantly. Major Nakamura, the same commander we'd had since leaving Japan, had told the commanding general in Manila that he would be responsible for taking care of the guerrillas that were in evidence all over the region where we were stationed. He had groups of us standing against the jungle wall, easily visible in the light of the pale moon. A few of us were killed every week.

Ike was in charge of Jimmy and me and we had a certain section to patrol. The store where I had first read my father's letter became our headquarters. Stores of this kind were called *sari-sari* stores, and were everywhere. The woman who owned the store had grown a little used to us, and I tried to convince Jimmy that if we kept going there she would hear us speaking English and would get a message to the guerrillas not to try to kill us. The back wall of her store was against jungle so thick that nothing could penetrate it. Each time she looked over at us from the far wall where she leaned I smiled and tried to say something nice. "How are you tonight?" or "You should accept payment for the tea you give us." One night I walked up close to her and said, "We won't be here long, you know. The war

is almost over and soon you'll have your Americans back."
But she hardly ever answered.

"Leave the poor woman alone," Jimmy kept telling me.
"She thinks you're going to rape her or something. Stop
smiling at her. This is war, man, act your age."

All through basic training no one had asked us about our
backgrounds, so I guess I was getting a little complacent.
The other soldiers accepted us, and even when we did
interrogations it was generally believed that Jimmy and I
had gone to school in America, that we'd learned the language so well as college students.

During the first few weeks of the war we didn't see any
real action. We heard stories of large losses on other islands,
we heard conflicting reports of Japanese victories and de-
feats at the same locations. But in the Philippines, for the
moment, what we were faced with was a guerrilla war. I
know that in the old American war movies Japanese soldiers
always seemed adept at jungle fighting, but we were not.
Whenever Major Nakamura decided we were to be aggres-
sive, we lost men. When he sent us into the jungle, we
knew our losses would be high and the reality of the war
came home to us. But if we could stay at the *sari-sari* store,
if we could win the hearts of the people and have them like
us a little bit . . . In this way we were sure to survive.

Jimmy was much more conservative than I was, much
more pessimistic. He would never talk to the other soldiers,
would never offer an opinion when we had a little time to
ourselves, and would never drink sake. Because he kept to
himself he became a figure of awe in the camp, for most of
the soldiers were boys and what they liked best about the
war was the camaraderie they could find with their fellows.
Indeed, even with me, Jimmy's inclination was to keep
everything inside. He got more and more distant as time
passed.

One night, a week or so after Ike and Jimmy and I began patrolling the roads and pathways around the *sari-sari* store, something happened. There was still a little daylight left so we were at ease, standing near the entrance to the store and smoking. The woman had made some rice cakes and had them for sale on the counter when I walked in. She moved quickly toward the wall when she saw me. I remember my uniform was tight about the neck and the heat was terrible.

"I have not yet made Japanese tea," she told me. "Will you take the rice cakes instead?"

The rice cakes were sticky and soft, but I was hungry, so I took out my knife and cut off a corner. They were sweet.

"How much do I owe you?" I asked. "I insist upon paying. Taking tea is one thing, but cakes . . ."

"No, no. I made them for you. Take them and go."

I held the sticky end of my knife up and looked about the counter for something to clean it with, a cloth or a piece of paper. There was a price marked on the top of the cakes, but since we'd made the *sari-sari* store our headquarters, most of the people who lived nearby would not come in and the woman wasn't selling anything.

"We've been a bother to you, haven't we?" I said. "It's just that we want to come in here to get away from the jungle. To get away from the prospect of war."

The woman still stood far away, but said slowly, "They think I am your collaborator. I have not lived here very long and now everyone is suspicious of me. When the war is over I will have to find another place to live because you want to come and stand in my store. Please take the cakes and go. You are not safe here. The guerrillas will kill me too."

The woman stiffened when I took a step toward her, to try to explain. My knife was sticky so I held it high. "What do you mean?" I asked. "Don't they know we speak English when we come in here? Can't they see that I and my friends are different? I'll tell you something," I whispered. "I am really an American. So is one of my friends. This whole thing is a horrible mistake. We are victims too, just like you."

The woman's mouth was open, her eyes on my knife.

"Oh no," I said. "I just want to clean it off. Do you have a rag or something? An old newspaper?"

The woman was getting nervous and would not move, so I stuck the knife in its sheath, sticky as it was. "You see," I said. "A sensible man would have cleaned it first. A real soldier would never have done that. Now do you believe me?"

"What is it that you want?" she asked. "Why is it that you do not leave me alone? We are enemies, you and I. I do not want to be your friend!"

I stood staring at the woman for a moment then took out my wallet and laid a few large Japanese bills on the counter.

"I don't want your money!" she shouted. "If they find that here they will kill me! I am not your friend! Go away!"

I was surprised at the anger in the woman's voice and wanted very much to explain. Always before she had simply stood there, answering only with a yes or a no. But now she was shouting. And suddenly, while I was trying to think of what I could say, what I could do to show her that I was telling the truth, the woman ran to the counter. She grabbed the money and ran out into the street with it. Jimmy and Ike were standing there, surprised when they saw her, frightened by the noise she made.

"Hey!" said Ike. "What's going on? Where are they? Did they come in the back of the store?"

Ike unbelted his rifle and, before I could stop him, emptied its chamber into the woman's store. He fired through the open door and the brittle bamboo side.

"No!" I shouted, but it was too late. Jimmy too had begun to fire and the woman, completely hysterical now, threw the money into the air and began to scream. "Jesus, Mary, and Joseph! Help me! Help me!"

"Where are they?" Ike demanded, running up beside her.

Jimmy was in a crouch. He turned, turret-style, keeping his eyes on the edge of the jungle, his finger fastened across the trigger.

"Hold it! Hold it!" I shouted. "Nothing's wrong!" But the woman moved toward Ike, scratching his face when he grabbed her. He held her down with one hand and raised his rifle.

"Ike! No!" I yelled, but the woman screamed and twisted in his arms. Ike let the butt of his rifle bang hard, one time, against the side of the woman's head.

Jimmy and I shouted together but all of a sudden it was quiet again, our shouts stopping at the edge of the jungle, muffled there by the lack of movement all around us, by the still, quiet, humid night.

"What have you done, Ike?" I asked, coming up carefully beside him. He was down beside the woman's body, bobbing this way and that, trying to protect himself from whatever it was that was out there. Jimmy had gone inside the store and had come back holding his rifle low.

"They've gone now," he said. "Whoever it was is gone now."

Ike still held his rifle level with the floor of the jungle, but everything was so silent that he soon let it fall.

"What was it, Teddy? Who was there?"

Jimmy was asking me questions, but Ike was slumped over the woman's body, staring. "There were no guerrillas," he said.

"I tried to tell you," I told him. We were arguing about whether or not I should pay."

Ike put a hand on the woman's shoulder, shaking gently,

but she didn't move. The blood in her hair mixed with the dry dust of the path making me wish the rainy season would come. Then everyone could stay indoors.

"She's dead," said Ike. "I've killed somebody."

"No you haven't, Ike," I told him. "She was just mad about me paying for some cakes. She'll be all right."

Jimmy shoved his rifle hard into my hands and knelt beside the woman's still figure, trying to find a pulse. Ike had tears in his eyes and rubbed the dirty sleeve of his uniform across his face. The insignia on his shoulder folded and unfolded with the movement of his arm.

In a moment Jimmy stood and said one of us should go back to tell the others. "She's dead, but it was an accident," he told Ike. "I was watching and I know you didn't hit her very hard."

"Oh . . ." said Ike.

When Jimmy said she was dead, I took a closer look at the woman but she looked all right to me. She didn't look dead.

"You go back, Ike," Jimmy said. "Tell them there's been some trouble but not to worry. It's all over now."

Ike stood straight and walked away immediately so I sat with the woman myself, holding her thin wrist in my hand and waiting. Only a moment before she'd been begging me to leave her alone, to take what I wanted from her small store and get out. I should have listened. The large bills that I'd given her could easily buy much more than those cakes I wanted and the guerrillas would have been suspicious that she had so much money. She shouldn't have shouted though, she shouldn't have run. I saw some of the money lying nearby, so I picked it up and went back into the store. The bullets hadn't done much damage. Probably most of them had passed through and were lodged in the leaves of the jungle behind. As I stood there I was struck by the general simplicity of tragedy. How it can seem so ordinary, how it can come so quickly and then be gone. When I heard the voices of the major and others outside, I put the bills back on the counter. The least I could do would be to help pay for the woman's funeral. I looked around for something heavy to hold the bills down, to keep them from being lifted away by a light breeze if one came by.

*

SINCE memory is selective I hope the fullness of mine will be appreciated. I make no excuses for myself, for my actions and lack of understanding. It is clear that I was a stupid boy, insensitive and dulled to the vividness of the world in which I lived. But I remember everything: the cast of the woman's body as it altered the contours of the dust, the cooling cakes on her counter, the calmness of Jimmy, and the shaking shoulders of Ike. Perhaps if the woman had died more dramatically I would have been more moved than I was. Certainly the occasion was dramatic enough, but her actual death was so sober, so much within the realm of what soldiers usually saw. There was no noise when the rifle hit her head, and she sat down so gracefully, not like falling, but like sitting, like simply sitting down.

I have often thought that opposites, in a man, are like the two tips of a perfect horseshoe. That is, though they may indeed be opposites, in the general curve of things they are very close together. It is the only explanation I have for the way I am, for the way I have been over the years. I was thoughtless as a boy but I do little else but think now. I am filled with love for my son yet cannot express it whenever he is near. I have loved only one woman in my life, but have often stayed with another. I think all men are like that. All mankind is. I remember Ike as our manager, how sweet he was and how he stumbled about. He always went on jobs with us. He'd sit at a table as close to the band as he could get and he'd keep the beat with his body, his involvement in our music sometimes reaching epileptic proportions. Yet after he clubbed the woman to death with the butt of his rifle, another angle of him began to appear. He stayed very close to Major Nakamura and became quite serious about infractions of the rules. Jimmy and I continued to keep watch, staying as much as possible to our silent selves, but Ike was transformed. He carried the major's clipboard and stayed up late at night studying the terrain, coming up with all kinds of possible theories as to where the guerrillas might be. He became the major's aide and lost his popularity with the troops. Though most of the rest of us wanted to stand our ground, with Ike's help the major finally decided that into the jungles we must go, that we must meet the bandits on their own ground and destroy them.

Jimmy, in his way, was madder at Ike than I was when we marched out to try to force our first encounter. In that part of the Philippines the jungle was thick, so an advanced troop of us would cut a patch of brush away, then the rest of us would move up and the work force would rotate. We forayed only one hundred meters into the jungle that day and when we returned we were exhausted and bitten all over by mosquitoes. Jimmy took Ike aside and tried to reason with him, but he could not. He learned only that after the woman's death Ike had told the major that we were Americans, and that though we could be trusted, we might certainly be more useful to the war effort than we had been so far.

Major Nakamura sent troops out in search of the guerrillas daily, and in a few days we found them. Cutting through the jungle, one of our fellows found a path, and so all quiet and with bayonets fixed, we began a real patrol. We walked single file, rifles high. On the tip of my bayonet I could see the dried cake that had cost the woman her life.

The guerrillas waited until we were all within their range and then attacked us in a methodical manner, firing down upon us from the surrounding trees. For a moment we stood there shouting at one another, then each of us pushed himself through the thickening brush at the sides of the path and fell to the fertile earth. I dug my way in and remained still. For a moment I could hear the chatter of the guerrillas, talking high up in the trees, and then everything was quiet.

Only Ike was with me on patrol that day, and I didn't know if he'd been hit. He'd been leading the patrol and I'd heard his commands occasionally, but it had been days since I'd actually seen his face. Every time we'd tried to talk, the dying posture of the *sari-sari* store woman had come between us. Through Ike's eyes I could see her limp body falling. In mine he could, no doubt, see that we had been in no danger.

Though I sensed movement about me I did not look up or move. I was sure that the guerrillas must have seen us burrowing in, but they neither shot at us nor slid down out of the trees to push their blades through the backs of our thin summer uniforms. The quiet was so complete that I remember thinking that the forest animals, the snakes and various birds, must have been scandalized into silence. The only thing unaffected was the wind. It nudged at the quiet edges of my uniform.

Even the darkness fell strangely that night. It fell upon the tops of the trees, then seeped in slowly, like a fog. And just before it finished drawing its black purse strings around us, there was fire from the trees and several shouts from the ground. Little lights the lengths of cigars shot out of the woods at angles. And with the resumption of the awful sound, I stood up. I imagined that the barrel of my rifle had mud in it and would not fire, so I kept it at my side. Most of the fighting was taking place toward the front of the patrol. At my end the velvet night seemed to have rolled in more thickly, giving me better cover than the others had.

When the fighting was hottest I stepped darkly through the trees and back onto the path. No one would expect me to be there. I waited until the next volley and then took a few quick steps to my left, bumping into the forest wall, but generally staying on the path. The shouts were coming from behind me then, for I was leaving. A flare whistled treeward and lit the guerrillas like a lightning flash, letting the Japanese soldiers shoot at the solid shapes that they saw. I took the opportunity to empty my clip easily into the chorus of sound, then to notice the way the path wound and to run.

I know that the popular cultures of both my countries would despise my actions. I could have saved myself, I suppose, in American eyes, by turning the barrel of my weapon on my fellow Japanese and having the Filipino patriots welcome me to their troop. Or I could have had honor in Japan by standing my ground and trying to kill as many of the enemy as I could. The truth is, had I been in the American army I might have done something like that, but as it was I simply slipped away. It wounded me to do what I did, but how could I have done otherwise? The eyes of the guerrillas were deep and steady, so sure that they were right. And the Japanese boys had their honor to hold on to. The spirit of the Bushido, the way . . .

I timed my steps to the sound of the gunfire and was able to get several hundred yards from the action in an hour. It was clear that at first light the small battle would be over. The guerrillas had the upper hand and only those who had managed to crawl away would survive. I thought of Ike, all unhappy about the woman whose life he'd taken, all military in his attempt to order his own life after that. If this had happened before he'd hurt the woman, he might be here with me now. But, of course, he could not want to survive if the others did not. The idea that we should be foraging around in these foreign woods was his, so he could not survive it.

I found a wide spot in the path and slept until gray dawn came to the tops of the trees. The gunfire behind me had stopped during the night, but as I woke I did hear, once more, a dozen shots carefully aimed.

When I reached the camp Major Nakamura was happy to see me but wondered how I had managed to get back. Surely, if I had returned, he said, we could count the whole thing a Japanese victory, if only by the margin of one. I hung my head and nodded, so the major patted my shoulders as if to relieve my fatigue. He knew how to praise as well as to punish. Now, he said, the guerrillas would think twice about stopping the Japanese army from carrying out its tasks.

After the major went off silently to grieve, some of the others came around and asked me to recount the battle for them, to tell how it all took place. Even Jimmy was inching toward my side. I held my head up high and spoke as if refreshed. "It was simple," I told them all. "We waited until morning and saw their silhouettes in the clearing sky. They were the solid shapes in the brittle branches of the trees."

*

Major Nakamura made me his aide. News of our encounter with the guerrillas reached the Manila headquarters, and soon we received instructions to desist, to worry about the open areas of the cities and towns where we were stationed, but to let the guerrillas stay in the woods, to give them that terrain as their own. We waited a week for Ike or any of the others to return and then we were ordered to move, transferred southwest to the province of Bataan. There were prisoners there and we were being called to guard them. The guards they had, it seemed, were in need of some time to themselves, a bit of open warfare for their psychological well-being.

Jimmy grew more silent in the days after Ike's death. Now that I was aide to Nakamura we rarely saw each other and by the time we got to Bataan I was too busy to worry about what he thought of my miraculous return. If he knew I'd run, I wasn't ashamed. If he was beginning to feel we should shoot like all the other Japanese, that was his problem. While working for the major I was assured of staying away from the front, and because I had survived such a brutal battle, I had all his confidence. I carried my clipboard, the same one Ike had used, and I walked about the camp doing my duties. Jimmy spent his free time with his face pressed against the wire, staring in at the poor prisoners of war.

Most of the prisoners at Bataan were American, and because of my duties as aide I often came in contact with them. The conditions under which the prisoners lived were bad. Many people in America are still convinced of the brutality of the Japanese, but part of it was that we simply didn't know how many prisoners there would be, we didn't have the tools to handle them, not enough food, not enough housing. And running a camp was hard work. It was easy to get angry.

When I came into contact with the prisoners, I kept my knowledge of English to myself. I was responsible for supplies and security. When I walked among them my heart went out, but what was I to do? If I told them I was one of them they would despise me, and there was no way they could help me get back home. If I told them merely that I spoke English they would want to talk to me and the quaver in my voice might give me away, letting them know the feelings of sympathy I had for them and weakening my position with the major.

One day when I got to Major Nakamura's office there

was a man from Los Angeles standing at tired attention in front of him. The man was the commander of a new group of prisoners, and had presented the major with a list of demands for better treatment, with requests for a change of diet, for better toilet facilities, for a place that the men could use for physical exercise. The American did not know it, but Major Nakamura was embarrassed. He'd been an elementary school principal before the war and had recently wondered aloud whether he'd ever be back in the school again. The man spoke to the major through an interpreter, a Filipino whose face did not change no matter what was said.

"He's a prisoner. Tell him not to forget his position," Nakamura told the man to tell the American. "These Americans . . . If we Japanese were being held captive we'd know how to act."

"War has rules," the man told the American. "Obey them."

Major Nakamura had gained a wide and unreasonable reputation as a disciplinarian but in truth he was a meek man, a man whose mind was set on surviving the war as much as mine was. He wanted to get home to his wife and family once again, to busy himself with the dainty discipline of the elementary school. Still, he knew belligerence when he heard it, even if the language used was English, and as the man from Los Angeles talked on the major got madder.

"Watch out," he said. "I have my orders. I will not have rowdiness." But when the man heard the translation all he did was laugh. He had not been a prisoner long. He still had a modicum of meat on his bones.

"What?" said Major Nakamura.

The interpreter looked from one man to the other, but neither spoke. "He didn't say anything," the interpreter told the major.

"He laughed. Doesn't he know that his life is in my

hands? Tell him not to laugh. Tell him if he laughs again I'll kill him. See how he likes that."

When the interpreter repeated what the major had told him, the man from Los Angeles kept quiet, but in a moment he said, "Obey the international rules for keeping prisoners," and he turned to try to leave before the major had said he could go.

"No!" shouted Nakamura. "You can't go until I give the order! Have you no sense of the way things are, of the relationship between conqueror and defeated during war? Don't you know how you are supposed to act?"

The major shouted and the guards at the door pushed the man back into the room. He sighed and said nothing after that, but he stood with his hands on his hips.

"Arms akimbo!" the major shouted, suddenly looking at me. "Japanese people hate arms akimbo! He knows that too, doesn't he?"

The Filipino interpreter had lost the line that the major was taking and when the major ordered the man to put down his arms the interpreter told him to surrender his weapons.

"We don't have any weapons," the man said. "We just want fair treatment. Tell him we just want fair treatment."

The interpreter told the major what the man had said, but by this time things were completely confused. Only I knew what was really going on, but I didn't want to talk, didn't want to tell this man that not only was I a fellow citizen of his, but I was from the same town, perhaps the same stretch of city.

"I will not tolerate arms akimbo," Major Nakamura told the man very slowly. "It is something I will not have." He was leaning over his desk and speaking directly to the man now, the interpreter pushed aside. Out in front of the room where we were talking, the American soldiers of the man's company were waiting in the dust. The sun beat down on them but the guards would not let them come into the shade. Everyone could hear the major yelling. When I looked through the window I could see Jimmy standing near the tired, defeated Americans. He had a rifle slung over his shoulder and was staring at the group and at the window where I watched him.

"Maki," the major shouted. "Come here. Maybe you can make this man understand."

"I'd prefer not to speak to him in English," I said. "It will undermine my effectiveness later."

"He's standing arms akimbo, look at him. Tell him to stop. That is what I can't stand about Americans. They are defeated but they act as if somehow they are better than we are. It's too much."

"The major wants you to put your arms at your sides," I said quietly, looking at the American directly for the first time. "He feels that your posture is defiant and would prefer that you act the part of the conquered soldier rather than that of his equal."

The man from Los Angeles was startled at what I'd said, but without comment he dropped his hands to his sides and then looked back at Nakamura.

"That's good," Nakamura said, talking to me. "Now I want you to put this man and his men in separate housing. We might make an example of this man. It seems every time I look through the fence I see someone standing arms akimbo. I want this guy in the center of the yard for a while. The heat will make him lower his gaze when he speaks to a Japanese officer."

Without looking at the man from Los Angeles again I went outside and told the guards what they should do. The American soldiers were all about my age. They'd been prisoners for a long time, but had been transferred in from somewhere else. When Jimmy heard that the group's leader would be kept in the center of the yard he looked at me, but when the time came he lowered his rifle and marched them away. The whole thing was disgusting. Major Nakamura had been milder in the jungle region than he was here and I had some trouble now, picturing him as an elementary school principal. Jimmy and I had been with him for the entire time we'd been in the Philippines and until this day he had not raised his voice, either at a prisoner or at a soldier of his own.

A day passed and the major still made the man from Los Angeles stand in the center of the courtyard. At times it seemed that he wasted more energy than the man did, constantly getting up and walking to the window to see if his prisoner had moved. Jimmy and five others were made to guard the man in rotation, night and day, and though the man was sometimes allowed to sit down, the major had gone out and drawn a circle around him saying that he'd be killed if he stepped or fell across the line.

A few days passed and the man from Los Angeles seemed to grow more defiant. His men could see him when they walked about their barracks and he seemed to take strength from the shouts that they gave him, from the sentimental, football-field mentality that they had. The major had cut the man's rations to a minimum so it was surprising how long he lasted. After the first few days I could tell that the major wanted the affair ended, for he had seen in the American a willingness to see it through. He sat at his desk sitting tall so that he could see the thin shape of the man's head, the way it waggled occasionally all loose on his still shoulders. Unable to sleep, Nakamura would rise from his mattress and stand at his window in the humid darkness just to see the slumped shoulders of the man in the moonlight. I knew, on about the fifth day, that if the man did step across Nakamura's line, the major was ready to kill him. The body of the *sari-sari* store woman had made the major retch, yet now he was willing to murder this man over a test of his will.

Late one night when the major was at his customary position, a worried look upon his face, nose pressed against the dirty glass of his office window, he saw something that broke the stalemate of the situation. Jimmy was on duty, standing facing the tall American, his rifle loosely held in his hands. Nakamura's eyes were rimmed red, I am sure, yet they were keen, and what they saw was Jimmy's hand coming up and something passing between it and the American officer's mouth. The major got out his field glasses and watched for the movement again and saw the brown band of a Japanese candy bar folded and tucked back into Jimmy's pocket. He was beside himself. He paced his room furiously for a few moments, then sneaked out his side window and came around to the general barracks where I and the others were sleeping.

"Psst," he said. "Everybody up. Keep quiet, don't turn on the lights." He sneaked around from mat to mat shaking our shoulders and whispering in our ears. "What we have here is mutiny," he told me after I was finally on my feet and awake. "Your friend has been feeding the prisoner. He has been supplementing his strength with Japanese candy!"

When we heard what the major was saying we looked at one another. "Get your guns and let's go," the major whispered, so we stepped behind him, silent as snakes, and wound around the side of the barracks until we were gathered in the gray courtyard a few meters away from them. I could hear English spoken softly, just a word or two, before the major stepped forward and shouted, before a switch was thrown that flooded the entire area with light.

The major marched forward and slapped Jimmy as hard as he could across the face. "Scoundrel!" he shouted. "Traitor!"

Jimmy fell down, but got up immediately, blood coming

a little from his lower lip. Everyone's eyes were still trying to adjust to the light.

"Empty your pockets!" the major ordered, but Jimmy stood swaying a moment, so the major hit him again. The American officer looked on. His face had changed in the five days since I'd seen him closely.

"You," shouted the major, "will be shot! And you," he said, turning to Jimmy, "will do the shooting!"

The major pushed his own hand into Jimmy's pocket and then carefully smoothed out the creases in the crumpled candy wrapper.

"Where were you born?" the major screamed, looking straight at Jimmy.

Jimmy paused, then said, "Los Angeles." He spoke in English and silenced the already dead-quiet crowd.

The major looked from one to the other of them. The American inside the circle was skinnier than he had been in the office the week before. If Jimmy'd given him candy he couldn't have given him much.

The major turned to all of us, the candy wrapper held up above his head. "We have a traitor in our midst," he said. "Yamamoto even speaks English when he is asked a question in Japanese." He stood a moment until his hands began to shake. His fury had forced his thoughts from him, but finally he shook his head and said, "In all my years as a school principal I never ran up against anything as awful as this."

The major was in charge but was out of control. The American officer had been crouching when we'd approached him but was able to stand, his long legs bringing him high above the rest of us. Jimmy still held his rifle on the man, trying to act the part of the proper guard. When the major regained himself he looked a long moment at Jimmy. He raised a short finger and pointed at the prisoner.

"Shoot this man, Yamamoto," he said. "Shoot him now."

The American seemed to know what was happening for all of a sudden he backed out of the major's circle and took a step or two to his right.

"Wait," he said.

The major's finger followed the man a moment, then he lowered it and called my name. I had been standing in the very back of the group of newly awakened soldiers. When he called me I felt a chill, though I was sweating and though the night was hot.

"Yes, sir," I said, softly beside him.

"Go to the barracks and bring a blindfold. Bring something with which to pin it behind this man's head."

"Wouldn't it be better to wait, major?" I asked. "In the morning perhaps all this will seem less serious."

"We will resolve it now," the major said. "You Americans really stick together, don't you?"

"Yamamoto merely felt sorry for the man, I'm sure. Really, he's as Japanese as . . ."

"Go!" the major said, swinging around, red-eyed again. "Or maybe, Maki, I'll find myself another aide as well."

I jumped a little when he shouted at me, but stepped away quickly while he turned his attention back to the two Americans. In his office it was easy to find the blindfolds, but I held back a little, hoping that time would cool the major off and maybe save the life of the man from Los Angeles. I could see them standing, waiting for me, through the window. Jimmy had been so stupid. In another day the major might have let the man slink back with the others, and that would have been the end of it. Now he was decisive, had locked us all on his course. As the men were waking up, they began to chatter and he didn't stop them. The American in the center of the circle was gauging his chances as slim, I'm sure. Even from the window I could see him bobbing about, his feet nervously scraping back and forth across Nakamura's old line.

"Maki!" the major shouted, so I went back fast, the whole box of blindfolds in my hands.

"Surely sir . . ."

"Tie the blindfold quickly."

I walked up to the shaking soldier and held a blindfold up to his eyes.

"Wait," he said. "I'll be good."

He tried to turn his head away from me so the major had a couple of the others hold him until I could secure the thing tightly behind his neck. "Try not to worry," I whispered.

Before the major turned to poor Jimmy again, he had another idea. He called to the guards who walked the ground around the American barracks, and told them to bring all the prisoners out.

"We'll let them watch," he said. "One lesson and we won't have a bit of trouble for weeks."

The guards were afraid to go inside the building where all the Americans were sleeping, so they shouted first, ordering those on the inside to turn on the lights. It took nearly ten minutes for the prisoners to be brought, single file, out into the courtyard, but when they were lined across from us the major seemed satisfied and drew another circle around the poor man, using the tip of his boot. All the Americans watched in sullen silence.

"Yamamoto," said the major.

Poor Jimmy had been standing there all this time, weakly holding his rifle. He was such a silent man, such a private one, that even during this moment, even when the essence of confrontation was upon him, he remained within himself. He had his rifle and it struck me that he might murder the major instead. He might turn the thing on us all.

"Yamamoto," the major said once more.

Jimmy walked a ways toward the major, then back near where I was standing with the wilting prisoner.

73

"It was only a candy bar," he said. "An extra one. Nobody wanted it."

The major walked to the prisoner and turned him around so that he was facing the others of his kind, all of them standing there in their drab Japanese issue, their poor pants all high water, the sleeves of their shirts too short.

When the major touched him the American said, "Ahh." Then with all the timbre gone out of his voice, all of its character missing, he said, "Please . . ."

There was no noise now, no talking. All eyes, those of the Japanese soldiers and of the American prisoners, were on Jimmy. The major made all of us stand at attention, then he backed away from the prisoner and waited.

Jimmy walked up to the man and said, "I'm going to have to shoot you now." He held his rifle to the man's head, its barrel just touching his clumsily cropped hair. Time passed. The American shook. I, in my position at the edge of the platoon, was holding my breath. The major did not move. Only Jimmy, absurdly, seemed calm. When he put the rifle down he turned back toward us and unbuttoned the top button of his shirt at the same instant.

"No," he said, very calmly and in English.

When the prisoner heard him he jumped a little and all of the other Americans began to talk.

I remember Jimmy had a slight smile on his face. When he spoke he broke the tension so completely for the Americans that their words came out harshly at us, like taunts. Major Nakamura stood still as the noise slapped against his ears. His face was red again, but this time he was not locked in indecision. He pulled his side arm from its holster and, walking over to where Jimmy was, put the barrel of it to Jimmy's temple and fired. Jimmy's smile did not leave his face as the small-caliber bullet passed through his brain. He seemed to stand an instant longer than he should have, then he fell at the feet of the blindfolded soldier, who, when he'd heard the shot, had nearly fallen himself.

No one moved. I remember thinking at the precise moment of Jimmy's death how hot it was and how odd the events had been that led him to the end of his life, here in the Philippines, far from the streets of Los Angeles, far from increasingly evil Japan. We were all frozen into the postures that the sound of the shot had put us in. The major held his handgun in the air where Jimmy's head had been. The voices of the Americans sank into the walls of the jungle and the prisoner stood, knees locked, in the center of that awful circle. Perhaps Nakamura was mad then, for he moved before any of the others did. He picked up the rifle that Jimmy had let tumble when he died and held it up to the stone-still troops. His handgun still hung from his limp other wrist and he waited, looking right at me.

"Maki," he said, finally. The awful rifle blurred to my vision but nevertheless danced before me, like a cobra.

I didn't move, so he walked over to where I stood and placed the rifle gently in my hands. "Your turn," he said. "Save yourself. Shoot him."

He was coaxing in the way he spoke to me and I could detect no anger in his voice. Jimmy's body lay before the American he was to have shot. His mouth was pursed as it was when he played his trumpet. I was walking, before I realized it, up to where the soldier stood, his back to me. The rifle's chamber was full but there had not been time for the tension of an execution to build once more. I raised the gun when the major took a step backward, away from me. It had a hair trigger, not connected to the weight of the moment. The man seemed relaxed before me and the Americans on the far side did not seem hostile to my action. There was a languid sense of levitation in me and I closed my eyes. I seemed to float. And I did not come back down to earth immediately. Not even with the sound of the report.

*

TWO

THE old tea teacher, the one in attendance at Kazuko's wedding, found me wandering the side streets of a section of Tokyo not far from where she lived. I was wearing my soldier's uniform and walking slowly, circling, trying to let chance decide whether or not I would ever see her again. Would she welcome firsthand information concerning the death of her husband? Would her mother want to know exactly how her son had died?

I don't know what decisions were made which allowed my return from the war so early, discharged and with no punishment pending, but it happened, and barely a month after the awful events of the evening I have just described. How old was the war then? Not a year certainly, for it was summer and I remember wiping perspiration from my forehead, upon my return to Tokyo, quite as often as I did in the war zone. Soon my uniform took on the darker circles of excess sweat, and soon, with my money gone and only memories to accompany me, my thin exuberance for life began to show signs of exhaustion. I was having trouble with my senses. Rather than the war-ready city, which everyone saw, I began to see before me the dead and hollow mouth of my endless future. Rather than the driving sounds of Tokyo, I began to hear the shots and shouts of the jungle guerrillas ringing in my ears.

76

I'm not sure how long I traveled, sleeping, when I could, down under Meguro bridge, but I like to think that even if the teacher had not found me I would have come to, of my own volition, and begun my life once again. It is true that there were others like myself, under all the bridges of the city, but they were the broken, not the injured. They were the vagrants of the war and I was not like them. They had lost their minds while I was merely escaping the ghosts of my immediate past. I had discovered that visions of my dead friends would not venture down the embankments and under the bridges with me. Images of Jimmy and Ike, like those of the *sari-sari* store woman, waited up on the real street where real people lived.

But one day I found myself talking to the old man who was Kazuko's tea teacher, found him questioning me about the condition of my person, found myself letting him lead me away to his narrow house and letting him bathe me among the tea bowls and tools of his art. I did not speak much then but I remember that he burned my uniform for me and in that ritual took away my credit under the bridge, my familiarity, my face. He shaved the beard from my chin and wrapped me in a summer *yukata* and fed me lightly before taking me to Kazuko's gate and making me knock. When Kazuko's mother answered the door he was gone, I am sure, but my calico cat stood at her side. It gave a silent meow and stepped down between my legs.

When Kazuko's mother saw me it was early August, three years before the Americans perfected their Manhattan Project and ended the war. She wept and called her daughter, who came from the inner chambers of the house. They had got word of the two deaths in their family and had lost their old grandfather with the news. I looked thin and tired, I know, yet I was clean and quiet when they pulled me from the empty street and into their lives once more. They did not, immediately, ask me questions about the details of their losses. Photographs of Ike and Jimmy stood on the altar in the far corner of the room, but my photograph was gone. Kazuko's mother, from the beginning, chattered on about tea and *sembei* and moved about the house as if at the edge of her dotage. Kazuko, though, sat staring at me and I at her. In me she must have seen the truth of my experience, for her eyes held the sadness I reflected. In her I saw the same beauty I had known, the same magnetic skin and face, but I also saw, alas, that she was full with child. Jimmy and I had been gone since late in the month of January and Kazuko had lived, most of that time, in the belief that her young husband could not die while she carried his child within her, his legacy, his thread to the continuing world. Had she, I wonder, told him of the slow expansion that her body was making for him?

There was no question that I would take up residence among them once more. It did not occur to either of them to ask about my early dismissal from the insane activities of the war. Kazuko's mother seemed absentminded about the loss of her son, and Kazuko took Jimmy's death with the forbearance and stoicism by which she was bred. Her pregnancy was the point around which they both lived, and each evening, when we sat listening to the war news or reading of Japanese victories at sea, Kazuko's mother would knit. She made small sweaters and boots and jackets that were gradual in expanding size so that when she held them up to us we were able to laugh at how quickly the child would grow, we were able to imagine him and find his progress noteworthy.

Kazuko was widowed and I had been sent away from the war so early, don't you see? It was no violation of friendship, no infidelity. Kazuko and her mother worked in war factories and were gone from the house each day, leaving me alone among Kazuko's things, among the accessories of her normal life. I used to stand at the altar, when they were away, holding some article of hers and staring into the two young faces in the photographs, the ones that I was so quickly outdistancing. I existed and they did not. I had grieved too much to feel any more guilt or to wonder if what I was about to do was wrong.

I had taken to holding the calico cat tightly, each day, so the night I finally went to Kazuko, it should come as no surprise that I carried my cat as protection against her sending me away. Kazuko's head was on a hard sand pillow, her arms straight at her sides under the thin blanket. The tatami that I walked upon gave quietly under my feet but the floor was not depressed by me, did not sink deeply in that part of the house, making each foot the center of pools as the tired tatami in the front room did. I had cleaned the cat for the occasion, had washed it on the cool back step and spent an hour with it on my lap, drying it under the warm shade of the small fig tree. Though the cat's three-colored fur made it oddly visible in the dark room, it looked at first incomplete, as if I held in my hands the roundish pieces of a difficult puzzle.

Kazuko was awake when I knelt beside her, but she did not turn her head toward me, so I began squeezing the cat a little, to make it purr louder, the surrogate voice of my passion. Kazuko was covered by the thinnest of sheets and when finally I lifted it away, I was forced to release the cat and the cat immediately went in where I would have gone, next to her oddly shaped body. The cat's head was up across her belly, its feet and stub tail right where I wished to sit, and even after I lifted the cat away, it stood, still purring, at her head. I could hear the cat clearly and I could hear Kazuko's mother sleeping in the far corner of the room. Her mother's feet were visible to me but her head passed through the door and into an antechamber, a warmer, smaller room, which she entered so oddly in order to gain a sense of privacy.

Discretion keeps me from mentioning too closely the particulars of our encounter, but I undid the loose knot of her obi and I remember noticing how wonderful the feeling of her flesh was against my own. Kazuko's breasts touched my hands timidly, but after that her abdomen rose like a fine round hill in some peaceful land. Momentarily I decided that what I was doing was wrong and I would have moved to leave if she had not said, "None of the women in my family have been large or difficult while bearing children. We have always been discreet of body," and so I stayed, and while Jimmy lay in the dust of my memory his living child moved a little under my hand.

"Come," said Kazuko. "I cannot be hurt by you. Nothing is wrong."

I think a normal man, one not injured as I had been, might have stayed his hand, but I did not. I moved across the vastness without hesitation, taking no time. I was not concerned that the noise we made might wake her mother or that my blind proboscis might bump the child, hurting some part of it. Rather I came to her as I might have had we truly been alone. The calico cat had quieted but still stood, sentrylike, at our heads. It watched us through its empty eyes, not purring now, not holding any thought, and from its blank reflection I took my rhythm. We were quiet, a little, and we were not untender with each other. Kazuko's eyes were open like the cat's and as I held myself above her I was able to look, for a while, at both pairs of eyes watching me. Kazuko was watching the contours of my face with such passive beauty that I knew that she was accepting everything she saw there. She would not judge me, would not question my survival. As I held myself above her I did not notice the awful August heat, but just at the end, when moistness was everywhere and her mother was turning in her sleep, what I did notice, what I did feel, was the conception of my own child. Minuscule though it was, I felt the bump of it, the linkage, the awakening.

I realize the risk I am taking by telling all of this. A pregnant woman, though she may have many fears, should be free, at least, from the fear of impregnation. Nevertheless, there are things a man can know without any proof at all. And as my seed set sail on its miraculous voyage I saw, in the cat's cold eye, that I was bathing the growing baby with the ingredients of myself and that he would be a mutation, a hybrid; Jimmy's boy but Teddy Maki's too.

There, it is said. And my sanity is still intact. We were all half-people in the room that night. Kazuko and I had suffered losses, great parts of us dead with the deaths of those we had loved. Kazuko's mother, though her legs and torso were with us, kept her mind locked privately away in a room of its own. And Jimmy was half there, together with me in shared fatherhood. I had bombarded his baby with a million versions of myself and I could imagine, there in the dead quiet room, all of Milo's little half-brothers and -sisters missing their mark, falling and falling through the muddy universe and finally dying out, unnoticed, like thousands of insignificant little stars.

*

KAZUKO's mood with me was fine, cheerful and natural, from the morning after the night I have just described. For my part, I pretended normalcy, I spent my days, while they were away at their factories, summoning up a kind of controlled cheerfulness which I dished out with supper and which seemed to fool them. My days, my times alone, were still full of the wolves of the past but I kept them at bay. The punctual return of my loved one, each evening, created an impasse. My darker mood was waiting, biding its time.

I had formed the habit of leaving the house shortly before Kazuko's return, each day, of timing my walks so that I met her at certain corners. And one night, though I had never mentioned him to her or told her that he had led me to her house, she suggested that we visit her old tea teacher.

"The war has turned him strange," she said, "but though he is funny he is still great. You might begin patching the holes in your education. A Japanese boy should not be so ignorant as you." Kazuko enjoyed teasing me, for she knew it made me feel at home.

The *sensei*'s house formed a triangle with Kazuko's home and with our meeting place, and when we got there I could see perspiration at the edges of Kazuko's lips, on her temples and across her brow.

"*Sensei, Sensei*," Kazuko called, softly and on tiptoes, looking over his fence and into his garden.

I could see a dark figure through the glass, could see it move across the room behind the door.

"*Sensei*, it is I," Kazuko said, "come to pay my respects. Let me in. I too will be a teacher someday!"

In a moment the teacher's muffled voice came through the glass to us. "Go away!" it said. "I am busy! If anyone wants to study tea they can come back after the war. I am closed!"

Kazuko stood quietly for a moment but did not call out again. And before long she motioned me back away from the door. We could see his dark figure moving back deeper into the house but we walked completely around the corner before speaking.

"I would have shown him the progress of my baby," Kazuko said. "I would have introduced you to him as its father."

This little anecdote, this little story of the teacher, is evidence that Kazuko and I did our best to act the parts we played, to treat Tokyo as if she were a willing host. But though she tried to get me out each day, though her energy and cheerfulness knew no bounds, I found that more and more I wanted to stay within the confines of the house. There were no other young men for me to be with, unless I chose the dangerous spectrum of those under the bridge, and I had begun to encounter, occasionally, the stares of strangers. Why, I read in their looks, are you here? I appeared able-bodied, strong and young. Why then, they seemed to ask, was I not at war?

Kazuko and her mother were up easily each day, off to work while I was still dreaming, and soon I began, once again, retracing the accidents and events that had altered my life. With each passing week I grew more catatonic and thus the cheerfulness I pretended, when Kazuko and her mother were home, must have seemed all the more difficult to muster, all the more transparent to them. I grinned fiercely and laughed, but I was unable to modulate my voice when speaking. I never knew whether tears might stream when laughter was intended. I could not eat, so pounds dropped from me and my mobility, when I was alone, became greatly impaired. My mind had no traction, no grip. Days, weeks, were pushed together like bodies in a modern Tokyo train. I was sick and I might have died had it not been for an event which pulled me back up among the living for a little while longer.

Kazuko had been working in a factory that manufactured flags, and on the day of the event I will describe she and the other workers were told that the vaults were full and that they had nothing to do but wait while the specifications of the machines were changed. Clouds hung low over the city that day. The workers stood on the small street in front of the factory like prewar workers out for tea. They were engaging each other in a guessing game, wondering what next they would make, when a small air raid, so far as I know unknown to historians, began above them. Because of the low cloud cover the plane came into view only a few minutes before it unzipped its belly and laid its stillbirth into the gray sky. Kazuko said that when they first saw it they all thought it was one of ours. The pilot cut his engines and came in quietly, letting the high complaint that his motor made start again only when he was visible from the ground. And when they all looked up, their hands shielding their eyes from the glare, he was so close that they could actually see his face, his black goggles looking down at them.

One woman near Kazuko began to scream, but the rest of them just watched. The pilot seemed to move away when he saw them. He dropped his bombs on some buildings a kilometer away and then tipped his wings and turned. Kazuko thought at first that he'd seen they were civilians and had gone far enough off course to let them live, but that was not the case. He floated through the air awhile then made a wide arc and came back out of the clouds, releasing one last bomb when he was directly over their heads. While they watched, the awful wound in the belly of the airplane healed itself. This bomb did not fall so magically as the others had. It wobbled. Its nose seemed already to have pinned them to the ground for they could only look, none of them running, none crying out. The black-rimmed eyes of the pilot, the goggles round and reflecting, made it seem as though they were being attacked by an insect, not by a man. Kazuko had even seen the hand that shoved the bomb. She saw adept fingers pushing at the unwilling object and she thought she could see the extra white area around knuckles hard at work. She described the fingers that pushed the bomb as albino spider's legs, all evil and hairless. The bomb took forever to reach them, letting them know, in its quiet competence, that the airplane was higher than it seemed. They would all have died had it hit them directly where they were, but instead it was the roof of the factory and then the poor women who were busy altering the fittings on their machines, who perished. The rest of them simply stood still. Even when the thing hit, even when its awful explosion cracked their concentration and hurled them to the ground, they were catatonic. Debris floated through the air in slow motion, like flotsam. Pieces of wood and brick tore into the path around Kazuko, pinning her to the spinning earth. And Milo, deep within his own world, gave a kick that made her add her voice to the sound that seemed to be tearing the sky apart. And all the while those puffy cumulus clouds moved about them in their slow conceit. Kazuko watched the small airplane disappear into them, its wings wobbling once, like a wave.

The bodies of the fitting changers were brought into the afternoon light and laid on the street for everyone to see. They didn't know any of them and someone counted heads twice to make sure that all the regular workers were unharmed, that no one had sneaked back into the factory to see what work the fitters actually did, to try to learn the inner workings of her machine.

From the area where the main damage was done they could hear sirens, could see black smoke rising. They were told immediately that the enemy plane had been shot down over open water, that the pilot and bombardier were now dead for what they had done, their bodies floating downward like lazy bombs themselves, toward the bottom of the sea.

Soon a brigade of firefighters arrived, hurrying to soak the caved-in factory walls, to water down the sides of surrounding buildings. Doctors moved among them asking if anyone was hurt, and the bodies of the fitting changers, all heavy and uncooperative, were picked up by the women from the ambulance corps and taken away. Kazuko had seen one of the fitting changers going into the shop and had spoken mildly to her, saying, "It is nice that you can take our places for a while," but she had not been able to recognize the woman among the dead. Milo was still acting oddly inside her but she kept her discomfort to herself, though she couldn't seem to stand again. The bombing, she said, had awakened Milo and he was angry, kicking out at a world that would rock him so harshly as this. While the other women began moving about the charred flag factory, Kazuko remained where she was, her eyes fixed on the light garment that she wore, on the movement that her skin made, now and again, as Milo's foot tried breaking through her frail body and into the light.

"Someone is still down over here," one of the doctors said, standing above her but shouting back to some others.

Kazuko looked up into the eyes of an old man and saw that he had been crying. Was this his first bombing as well? Tokyo was prepared for what would come, but so far the rescue crews had had little to do.

Milo stopped kicking when the doctor knelt beside her. When he put his hands on her abdomen Milo seemed to shrink away, to hide in the far corners of her body so that she appeared to be less pregnant than she had been the moment before.

When the old doctor called again several others came, and by the time her first real labor pain started she was on a stretcher and being carried off the way the corpses went, off toward a long line of buses. Kazuko's benchmates and some of the others saw her and walked along beside her stretcher, holding her hand and crying, telling the doctor, "It is still too early," and whimpering. They clung to each other when she was finally loaded onto the bus, falling together in a standing collapse until the doctors and the bus driver laid hands upon their shoulders and guided them back toward the burnt-out building.

With all the commotion, with all the action around the bus, Kazuko decided that the best thing she could do was to remain quiet, so even when the labor pain returned she did not cry out. Though a few doctors got back on the bus, Kazuko and the corpses of the fitting changers were the only other passengers. When they began their slow movement, their trip off somewhere across Tokyo, Kazuko laid herself long on the stretcher, for the bus was not fitted with the normal seats and there was plenty of room. The doctors had tried to put all the fitting changers toward the back, but one of them was not far from Kazuko and she could see a pale hand as it fell from the blanket and reached toward the floor.

If Milo Maki was unhappy traveling so far with these quiet companions, he kept his displeasure to himself, and Kazuko began to fear that those first kicks may not have been in anger but in pain. Had he now wrapped his umbilical cord around his neck so that he'd not have to join such a ruined world? Kazuko called out to the doctors once but pain stopped her call just as it started. She was sweating and pressed down on some part of Milo's poor body with all her weight.

At first, when they left the factory, Kazuko imagined that they'd be headed for some hospital, but as she leaned up and looked out the bus window she noticed that they were now slowing, coming to a stop near where the main bombs had hit. Other buses were parked here and there and other doctors rushed through the ashes and smoke. Kazuko did not recognize the building, could not remember which direction, from her flattened factory, they had gone. But for as far as she could see the sides of the buildings were cracked open, their contents spilled into the streets. This was no machine shop, but a place where people lived, a human center of some sort. Blankets covered corpses all around the area, and lying among them were the wounded, women with one knee bent up or with a hand waving slowly in the air.

The doctors from Kazuko's bus opened the wide front door and began loading the covered bodies in around her. "Just hold tight," one of them said to her. "You've picked an odd time to add to the living." The dead filled the back of the bus and began building toward the front. Kazuko's labor pains came and went but Milo still wouldn't kick again, would not move around within her. From the other side of the bombed building came a parade of uninjured factory workers, two by two, each pair with a poorly postured dead woman slung between them. On most of the dead the black factory shirts were pulled away from their black pants so that a bit of skin was visible, all pale-looking and bloodless. The women who carried them struggled, one pair stopping altogether, abandoning a body for a moment to go and retch where the side of the building should have been, their vomit hitting the air and then falling on the dislodged bricks.

Even when the bus was full they did not move. The dead women were stacked with care, one on top of another, their palms falling open as if each was asking Kazuko to read her fortune for her. When all the windows of the bus were blacked out by their bodies Kazuko began calling to the doctors as they walked past the open door, but she could get none of them to come to her. "There is a baby coming here," she said, trying to keep the edge of pain out of her voice, indeed, trying to give her voice an uncomplaining ring, a sound that would so contrast with the awful agony around her that surely someone would hear. She thought that maybe Milo had turned within her, for she could feel the shape of him, his eyes pressed tightly against her spine, his head down. Were the sounds of the world audible to him? Could he take the option, now, before he took a breath of his own, to be stillborn among all this activity? To avoid a world such as this one?

The doctor who had first ordered her put onto the bus

was back and standing in the doorway. His tunic was stained only a little and when he spoke to her he was calm and smiling. "Are you still lying quietly? Are your pains rhythmic now? Shall we get you among living people to have your baby?"

"My baby will get the wrong idea of the world if he is born here," Kazuko said. "He would be born now if he thought the place was right."

The doctor came all the way into the bus and knelt by her side putting his hands near the round rump of Milo. When he turned and called through the door of the bus, the others, those standing nearby, had no trouble hearing him. "Can you walk?" he asked her. "Can you stand and come with me?"

Another doctor, younger and sadder than the first, came in and when Kazuko tried to move they both offered her their hands. Milo, as if cooperating, did not bear down, seemed to move higher up in her body to help her.

"The sight of you walking among the wounded will give them hope," the old doctor said. But Kazuko couldn't see any wounded then. Around the outside of the bus there were only stacks of blankets, waiting.

With the two doctors helping her, they moved around to the side of the building that had been chosen as the congregating point for those who had survived. The building had been a factory after all, and as they walked into the area of the living Kazuko could see, through the great and still standing double doors of the place, the machines that the women had worked. They'd been packing field rations, food for soldiers who could not come in at night, and the gooseflesh texture of cooked rice had broken through the tough sides of a thousand exploded cans and was strewn among the survivors. Some women were sitting among the rice and crying softly, but most were silent, waiting to be cleared by the medical team so that they could go home.

At a place where the survivors stood most thickly the doctors put Kazuko down. Here all the women were clean and unhurt. When they saw her perfect pregnancy, the fullness of it, many of them came to where she was and sat with their feet tucked beneath them, just as they would at the tea ceremony. They sat all around her and began to talk.

"When we heard the bombs coming some of us knew exactly what it was," one of the women said. "When your baby is born you can tell it the story of its first day. This side of the factory has more survivors. The heavy machinery kept the flying cans and falling ceiling away from us. It was the women on the other side, the packers and crate sealers, who had the worst of it."

The voice of the woman was cheerful and as she spoke Milo began to push again, as if he too got some comfort from the sound, some sense of the tragedy winding down. When Kazuko called out at the pain, she felt the women moving in closer, a few more joining the circle, until no one from the outside could have seen her. But as the pain of Milo's incessant pushing got clearer to her, the facts of the situation began to alter. The doctors who brought her there kept disappearing, the faces of the women who made up the circle changing, yet the order of their sitting became tighter and tighter, each time she looked, more solid. Kazuko was having her baby surrounded by a wall of strangers, all smiling, all chirping softly, like visiting birds.

When the doctors came back they had clean blankets for Kazuko to lie upon, clean pans with water and soap. One of them came up to her, leaned very close to her head, and began to whisper, saying, "The hospitals around here are full. The emergency rooms have bomb victims in them and the corridors are lined with the dead." He smiled as he spoke. He asked Kazuko to try to roll over onto her side.

One of the women had been given a cloth and began to

wipe Kazuko's face and forehead every few seconds. Milo's pushing was getting stronger, yet her body was gradually being lulled by the pain. The push and effort of Milo was becoming a little bit clinical to her, a matter of interest, but not so painful as before, no longer a trauma that she could physically share with him. In this way Milo, not yet born, was already growing distant from her, growing away, taking his independence as all men do.

One of the women bent so close to Kazuko's face that she was startled when her thoughts cleared and she was able to notice her. "Hello," the woman said. "Is this your first child?"

Kazuko nodded, so the woman and her companions bent closer. Kazuko could no longer see or feel the doctors, though she was confident that they were near, that Milo would be born into their capable hands. She thought she could feel her legs spreading, but she was not sure. The largeness of her stomach was a tempting place, a table on which she suspected many of the women wanted to rest their arms.

"Ah ha!" said the woman next to the woman who had been speaking to her. "If the baby is born under such circumstances as these, the baby will most certainly have a charmed and interesting life. It will be a baby of extremes."

Kazuko could see the faces of eight women but was sure that there were more, layered thickly behind the eight, like flower petals. She had lost too much of the feeling of what was going on, could tell only that there was movement, and she began to worry at the decreasing pain. Was it true that a mother who does not suffer with her child is a mother who will forever search for the ties which bind them? Kazuko wanted to ask the question of the women around her, but looked at them and asked instead, "Don't you think that we would all be better able to deal with our lives if we were to keep up the study of tea?"

The women all had their hands on her abdomen now,

not resting, but rubbing lightly. When she spoke of tea, a subject so distant from the one at hand, they looked at each other and smiled.

Kazuko said, "I know the birth of my baby is soon, but look around you. Buildings are beginning to fall, the enemy aims his bombs at the upturned faces of women. It is at times like these that tea comes to mind. The momentum of our traditions can save us."

Most of the women, Kazuko thought, did not look as if they were listening to her. Their heads were turned now toward the odd angle of her legs; each was trying to have a clear view of Milo as he emerged from that world into this. One of the women laughed and pushed the hair that had strayed onto Kazuko's forehead back away from her eyes.

Occasionally one of the doctors would ask Kazuko to push and she would try, halfheartedly, to make Milo move out into the air faster, but it did not seem to be helping much. The bulge that was her belly had indeed dropped as it was supposed to, but the staying power of Milo was strong. In a moment she realized that there was but one doctor in attendance, for when one of the women stood to stretch she saw the other doctor walking among the wounded across the pavement from her. Factory workers were still holding their hurt parts and calling out, though for the longest time Kazuko had not heard them at all.

"Push!" said the doctor. "It is the excess of pain that is making you dreamy. Push or your baby will not be born at all!"

For the next half hour Kazuko concentrated, the women urging her on, the doctor saying, "Yes, yes." Milo started moving as soon as Kazuko bore down. He seemed to be pushing when she did, resting too, when she turned her head to the side to look about.

"There," said the doctor. "A small cut and he's coming.

What will you call your baby? There are many new names and many good traditional ones as well." The doctor had stuck his head through the circle of surrounding women and Kazuko began to laugh. "Just another moment," he said.

She could feel the turning of her spine and she cried and saw the dramatic drop of her stomach. It fell much as the buildings around her must have, and she felt the body of her baby slide from her ever so smoothly and it was wonderful. Almost immediately her size was normal again.

Instead of the cry that Kazuko had expected, Milo's first sound was only a small cough, like the cracking of the seal on a too tightly closed jar. The doctor held Milo upside down for an instant, his face red and looking like dried rice cake. Kazuko saw his mouth turn from slit to circle, saw the way his lips quivered just before the first real cry struck the population of the bombed zone so ironically. His new chest and arms changed in color as he began to wail and the women and the doctor began to cry and smile and Kazuko did too.

"It's a boy," said the doctor, cutting Milo's umbilical cord and moving her placenta away.

"Milo Maki," she told them all. Kazuko took the baby from the doctor's heavy hands and tucked him under her shirt. Blood and liquid smeared her rib cage on the side where Milo lay. He would not take her breast for a while, though she pushed it all the way to the edge of those still quivering lips. His eyes were buried in wrinkles and smeared with such a slippery substance that Kazuko wondered what it was that made his birth so hard. He cried twice more, then settled down to breathing the way we all do, one breath at a time, not gulping, no longer worried about this new substance which came into his lungs and was, all of a sudden, so important to him.

Milo was very small but was healthy, and a few moments after his birth the doctor told Kazuko that there would be someone around soon who would take her, in an automobile, all the way to her home. She was simply to stay where she was, there on the ground. After Milo was out of view, after he had taken the nipple of her still dry breast in his mouth to give it training, the women and the doctor stood and stretched, letting the sun in a little. It was like the blossoming of a flower, the way each of them opened up like that. And when they walked away it was like autumn coming and Kazuko began to feel the chill and could see so clearly once again the devastation. She pulled her body up around Milo's and watched as the doctors and volunteers tended to the ever-present wounded. They had taken the time that was necessary to assure that at least there would be one new life here today, and now they were back to work. When Kazuko looked in at Milo he was asleep, and when she looked toward the area where her bus had been parked she could no longer see any of the dead, any of the bodies stretched out and waiting to go.

"May I see your baby?" asked a wounded woman who came up beside her quickly. She had only a slight wound really, a missing finger, the first one on her right hand, and she said she would have escaped injury altogether had she not seen the shaking of the roof and tried to warn her companions and coworkers by pointing up at it and crying out. A can of soldier's rice, its sharp tin edge as yet unbent by the creasing pliers, had not been slowed at all by the small resistance that her finger gave. She had found her severed finger in the dust of the machines, a few meters away. "Look," she said, after she had peered, for a while, into Milo's sleeping face. And it was as if she wanted to keep them even, showing Kazuko a bit of herself for what Kazuko had given her to see.

*

WHAT saves a man from the disengagement of his spirit is not a woman but a child. A woman can do battle against the forces that wear him down but it is the child who might actually and completely rescue him.

When Kazuko and Milo entered the house it was still too early in the day for her to be home had she done a full day's work. I was in the garden sitting upon a low stone bench, bent and staring at my reflection as it lay upon the top of the water, above the spotted carp. Kazuko came directly to me saying, "Master, your son is here," making me turn quickly out of my introspection. Kazuko looked pale and thin, yet she was so beseeching, and her gift was held out to me in such a delicate and gentle way that I jumped up, taking her into the house to rest and leaving my crimes and my guilt out in the garden.

I remember feeling a lightness of heart when I looked at my son for the first time, but more than that I felt a devastating hunger. So after I spread the *futon* and as Kazuko and Milo fell to quick and grateful sleep, I stepped into the kitchen and began to eat. I scraped rice from the sides of an old pot, using a wooden spoon. I lifted the tops off containers and quickly dropped pickled vegetables into my mouth. Kazuko's mother had bean curd ready and when I saw it I leaned down and bit the top of it, leaving a mark like one a rat might make, a scar across its surface and side. I ravished the bean sprouts, ripped whole strips of salt fish from the bones, and drank the *misoshiro* from its pot as if it were water. I ate rice cake that Kazuko had been saving for dessert and I found, under the floorboards toward the rear of the kitchen, a bottle of fine Chinese wine. I cracked the seal and put it back half-gone. And when I was spent I fell to sleep with my family, not once thinking of the war, of Major Nakamura, or of Jimmy and his little legacy beside me.

When we woke we realized that we had only a few moments to prepare ourselves for the return of Kazuko's mother. We seemed to wake all of an instant, and Milo, though he did not cry out, was busy working his mouth in ways that made me think he might. We quickly pushed the *futon* out of the way and positioned ourselves as we might for a family photograph, sitting close together in the front room.

We could tell that Kazuko's mother was tired by the noise the door made sliding in its groove when she opened it. She stood for a long while taking off her shoes, while Milo and Kazuko and I waited secretly. Most of the red had gone from Milo's face by then and we'd hurriedly cleaned him up and dressed him for her. He had fallen back to sleep though, and the white knit cap that his grandmother had made curled off the top of his head like an old man's nose.

"Mother," Kazuko called, not wanting to startle her when she saw us. "I'm home, come look."

Kazuko's mother stepped up into the anteroom but did not turn toward us. She wanted water on for tea and was miffed, I could tell, that tea was not ready, that Kazuko had not put water on when she'd arrived so early.

"Our factory was one of the ones bombed today," Kazuko told her. "Near us many people were hurt or killed."

Kazuko's mother stopped what she was doing and came into the room where Milo Maki slept upon the top of the table, all curled in his newborn way.

"Oh, my dear," she said. "You are not injured?"

But Kazuko did not answer, nor did her mother ask again. Her eyes had reached the pinched persimmon of Milo's face. "*Ah ra!*" she cried, dancing sideways a bit and then coming over and running her hand softly over the flat front of Kazuko's kimono. "When? Where?"

Kazuko laughed for a time, pointing up at her mother as she stood there above us. Milo sucked his seeded gums and opened his mouth once while Kazuko told her mother the story of the day, and soon Kazuko's mother picked him up lightly and began to sing to him even while Kazuko spoke. "*Sho-sho-shojo-ji. Shojo-ji no niwa wa. Tsun tsun tsukiyo de mina dete koi koi koi.*"

She danced with him through the small room, even over toward the tokonoma where the tatami was weak and the floor gave a little under her feet.

"He's had a long day, Mother," Kazuko said. "Try not to wake him."

Her mother danced with Milo into the other room, where she placed him on the floor and went about the business of laying out the *futon* in a proper manner, with crisp and clean sheets tucked under it. She had made new bedding for Milo. He had a tiny new pillow and a wonderful patterned top, and she knelt beside him when he retired, singing several songs that I had not heard since I was little and my mother sang them to me. She looked at Milo's small form sleeping there, at the way the blankets came up just to his chin, at his thick patch of black hair, all askew, like a poorly kept calligraphy brush. "Milo Maki," she said, messing up the vowels a little, and I felt giddy, fresh, anxious to watch him grow, for him to recognize me as his father.

*

THE first year of Milo's life was serene for us, but not for the city. Every day seemed to pass in photographic repose and I remember no events. At the end of Milo's first eighteen months, however, though Kazuko's mother went daily to her work at the uniform plant, Kazuko was still home with her baby. She had decided that she would stay with Milo long enough to see, at least, his robust flesh lose some of its baby tones, long enough to know, at least, that he knew her name and might call for her if, finally, she decided to work again.

The official word was that we were winning the war but

the sounds from the sky made everyone suspicious. Airplanes with spider-faced pilots like the one Kazuko had seen had been finding their way through our defenses often, and for a while the radio and newspapers reported the locations of their strikes. Milo and I sometimes heard the awful buzz of the unknown planes in the hours of the morning when we were wide-eyed in our beds but not yet ready to rise. And not long after that Kazuko's mother began giving reports each evening that there were certain areas of the city that had been burned nearly entirely away. Kazuko kept listening and wondering what she would do if she heard, once again, the dull complaint that she'd heard over her factory, the patient whistle of a bomb descending. But as each month passed the neighborhood remained as it had been before the war. Except fewer housewives gossiped on the streets, fewer pushcart merchants called out the names of their wares as they passed slowly by.

To spend the days alone, yet still in the presence of another human being, always under the simple gaze of our baby, made us try to set an example for him. "Milo," we would say, "it is wonderful to have you but there is a war on. You will be surprised later, when you find that life is not normally so poorly lived around us." Kazuko would make up little songs containing messages pertinent to a good life, and as she sang and danced throughout the house Milo would seem to watch and listen. He was a fat baby, yet from the folds of his face I detected an intelligent interest in the songs his mother sang, as if he were listening to the words.

Then one Sunday, though we had been cautious about taking Milo out of the house too often, we decided to take him to the Buddhist temple nearby. There were still monks living in the temple and there had been articles in the newspaper asking, wouldn't it be better if these priests, scattered throughout the country as they were, donned uniforms and were placed among the troops to uplift their spirits and offer parables? They had been stupid articles and had made Kazuko's mother laugh to picture the priests all dressed like soldiers, Kazuko's small and delicate battle flags sewn to their sleeves. Milo, hearing the unfamiliar sound of laughter, smiled slightly and then farted as he tottled along.

It was a cool but clear day, and as soon as we passed under the temple gate we saw, ahead of us on the stone path, a young priest sweeping, sending dust into the air around him and peering at the rocks to pick weeds with his fingers.

"Young priest," said Kazuko's mother, "what do you think of the article calling upon your kind to join the service? Do you think it justified?"

When he saw us the young monk picked up his cleaning basket and hurried off in the direction of the main temple house. He did not answer, and though the skirts of his robe danced up around his knees in the breeze he made, he did not slow down.

Kazuko's mother was holding Milo's hand and letting him walk slowly along the path beside her. We turned up the same path the monk had taken, and as we walked Kazuko reminded me of the story of our calico cat and how I had retrieved it from the arms of a gangster and how I'd suffered a real wound for my trouble. Kazuko's mother nodded as I walked beside her but she kept her eyes on Milo, her feet straight on the path. We walked up to the top of the small bridge that covered a carp pond and looked down into the open and waiting mouths of the beggar fish. "We will all be like that if the Americans win," Kazuko said, then she picked Milo up and stretched way out over the railing with him, hoping that he would see the fish and recognize that there were other creatures on the earth.

"Stop that!" shouted her mother. "You might drop him! Stop now!"

She pulled hard on the sleeve of her daughter's kimono and when Kazuko bent back up, her mother quickly took Milo away from her, appalled by what she had done. "Really Kazuko, there are limits," she said. "Talk if you must, but never lift a child toward an open pond! I know the war is hard on you but there are limits!"

Her mother was angry and walked quickly off the bridge ahead of us, taking Milo with her. And when we got to the main temple building Kazuko's mother was still punishing us by walking a meter or two ahead.

"Why don't you wait?" Kazuko called once, but her mother entered the big building and when we finally caught up she was feigning involvement with the Buddha image that sat before her, the light from its eyes so dull upon her face.

"The Americans are not going to bomb Kyoto," she told us. "I heard it at the bath the other day. They are going to concentrate on Tokyo. They have respect for Japanese culture and have decided not to bomb our best cities."

When I looked at Kazuko's mother I saw that she'd been crying, her tears falling down and wetting Milo's hair.

"I wasn't going to drop Milo in the pond, Mother," Kazuko said. "I just wanted him to see the fish."

"The ladies in the bath have been having an argument," her mother said. "Do the American bombs blow things up or blow things down? Try to remember. Is it better to hide in the back of your house or to run out into the street and get under a tree? I told them of your experience and they'd all like an answer from you."

Kazuko tried to take Milo's hand from her mother but she wouldn't let her. Milo looked toward Kazuko in the same way her mother did, as if he too expected an answer.

"I don't know," Kazuko said. "There is nothing to worry about, you know. They are going to restrain themselves. The ladies in the bath won't have to worry about it."

Her mother got mad again and said, "We are discussing,

not worrying. It is a simple question. Do they blow up or down?"

Kazuko stood staring at her and at the dusty Buddha sitting there so patiently. "Down," she said, finally. "If I remember correctly the bomb goes off on top of the object that it hits and the pressure from the explosion blows everything down. What difference does it make?"

"So if we were in the bath, if the ladies were in the bath, they wouldn't be very safe at all? They'd be hit by falling roof tiles and left dying and naked in the tubs. They'd be wounded and unable to cover themselves. Would they drown or would the impact from the bomb splash all the water out of the tubs?"

"The bath would not be a good place to be," Kazuko said evenly.

Her mother nodded briefly when she decided that there was no hint of condescension in Kazuko's voice, then she and Milo turned their attention to the Buddha and the relics that sat in cages all around them. There were old Buddhist hats and long chains of beads with tiny Buddha images impressed within them. Kazuko's mother said her favorite temple article had always been a human hair rope, coiled like a thick and silky snake, in a huge glass case in the far corner. I enjoyed watching the way she pointed it out to Milo, and Kazuko said she remembered her mother showing the rope to her, in the same manner, years and years before.

"Once I knew where the hair for this rope came from," said her mother, "but now I have forgotten. It was such a dramatic story that it seems impossible that I would forget it, but now I have. What do you make of that?"

When we had circled the inner walkway of the temple and were back in front of the bronze Buddha once again, Milo began to cry. Kazuko had full breasts and pulled her clothing around so that she could bring him to them, but her mother was still reluctant to give him up.

"Mother," said Kazuko.

"You'll drop him in the carp pond."

"He's hungry. I've milk for him. Everything's fine."

Kazuko had bared a breast and I was looking down at the bluish veins that ran out of her upper chest and down its slope. She found a small bench and sat with perfect posture, turning just a little away from the Buddha's cool eyes. She held out both her hands with enough authority so that her mother let Milo go to her. We watched as Milo's mouth let a seal of Kazuko's milk run around its edges, we listened to his lovely clucking. "He will be safe with his mother, I suppose," said Kazuko's mother, finally sitting down softly beside them.

While we waited there, Kazuko's mother and I watching the wonderful lightening of Kazuko's breasts, a line of seven Buddhist acolytes came in through the huge front door of the temple and began walking around toward the side. They were bald young men and walked single file, in identical formation. There was humor in their seriousness and Kazuko and I began to laugh. Each of the young men carried a hoe or a rake across his shoulder, as the soldiers did their rifles.

"Young priests, young priests," Kazuko's mother called.

The young men stopped. They had not noticed us sitting there and as they turned about, each just missed the one behind him with the dangerous tip of the tool he carried.

"We would like to have a word with you," said Kazuko's mother. "About the war. What are you doing here? Why don't you all go out and fight?"

The young men looked at each other, but then turned back and hurried away, so Kazuko's mother stood and called, "Come closer and look at my grandson. The Americans will bomb your temple and might kill us all. The blue veins of my daughter's breasts will be torn from her skin, spilling her milk onto the dirty streets. What good does it do, then,

preferred, clearly, over the coos and voices of his mother and grandmother, the singular and sterile company of a man.

*

ASIDE from the joy she took in her grandson, Kazuko's mother's only pleasure, during the war, was her nightly selection of a public bath. There were a half-dozen baths reasonably close to our house, and it was her job, each evening, to decide where it was that we would go. She carefully described, to Milo and Kazuko and me, the best qualities of each bath, speaking slowly and expertly, and it was our job to be attentive, to insist as much as she did, upon the importance of the ritual.

One evening, during the early spring weeks of the war's final year, she chose a bath some distance from our house and we set out in clean kimonos, Milo holding my hand and stepping along between his mother and me. Kazuko's mother was talking cheerfully, anticipating the bath for us all, when we turned a normal corner and discovered before us a part of the city that had been bombed. We slowed when we saw it, standing tentatively at its edge. It was not a large area, but there had been houses there only a few days before, and we'd been unaware of any such nearby bombing. The ground in front of us was cold gray and had been burned so evenly that there were few mounds of ash. It looked like a field in preparation for some kind of devilish crop, and we were afraid to cross it, afraid to step, with our clean *zori*, onto its awful crust.

It was odd to be walking in urban Tokyo and to suddenly find a newly made and open field. There was a warm wind about and as we stood there, hoping not to see a sight worse than that silent field itself, Milo began to laugh. He had been a docile child, a slow responder, but now he began pointing at the rubble, laughing, and even clapping his hands. "Ha ha," he said, in one of his languages, and I was forced to hold on tightly to his hand for fear that he might slip from my grip and go walking off into the ruins.

"Milo!" said his grandmother. "Stop it. People died here and we must be sad." But we could not control his joy. He smiled with such obvious delight that Kazuko and I looked quickly to see if any of the lucky neighbors, any of those whose homes were bordered by the burn, might be watching. We nodded our apologies to the sides of their houses and turned back the way we came.

"We'll go to another bath," said Kazuko's mother, using her body, as we retreated, to block Milo's view.

Had we seen the bombed area a few weeks earlier than we did, I think we would have been more distressed. By spring, however, the people in our neighborhood had adjusted to the probability of seeing such sights. They had prepared for them in conversation, they had heard descriptions of them from others, and, in a certain way, they had been looking forward to them.

By the time we reached the second of Kazuko's mother's baths Milo had turned inward again, but when we stepped inside the building he woke to the smell of the steam and the sound of the water. The woman who ran the bath sat high up in her cashier's box, just between the two doors leading to the two bathing areas. I could see that the men's side was empty and hoped, since male customers were few, that Milo and I would have it to ourselves the entire time. When Milo smiled at her the woman came down off her high stool and went in search of something for him, a candy or a treat of some kind. The women went ahead of us and, once inside the dressing room, undressed and stood with some other ladies, all of them waiting so that they could go into the bath together.

One of the rituals of my closeness with my son then was, of course, the public bath. And when Milo and I finally entered our section he had been given a sugar lump and I a large wooden box, a special tub in which I might place Milo, in which I might temper the heat of the water to suit his tender skin. Upon occasion Milo would go with his mother to the other side, but he did not like the constant clucking of the old ladies, the way his grandmother would hold him up for their fine inspection. When he was with me Milo knew that, though I bathed him well, he would soon be free to roam the tiled room as he might, to stay in the cloudy corners where I could barely see him, to imagine himself the child of those wastelands he seemed so attracted to, to think in English or Japanese and to try to understand why those languages, within him, were at war.

Yet though I bathed my son well it was the cleansing of myself that was paramount. I sat on the low stool and took a porous stone to the bottoms of my feet, so thoroughly scrubbing away the calluses there that I knew I would walk gingerly for an hour or two thereafter. I soaped my body in a way that made Milo laugh, and when I rinsed the soap away I quickly repeated the process, making Milo shriek with joy at the sudsy crown upon my head.

When finally I stepped carefully into the tub my body turned slowly red and for a moment I forgot Milo, abandoning him to his slippery play. I was lulled by the bath and thought, for a while, of home. I wondered what it was that would make whole families of good Japanese want to move, as my family had, to a country such as America. It had seemed at times, when I was there, that half of Los Angeles was made up of people like me and when I asked myself what they would be doing about the war I had to answer that surely they would fight, that their loyalties and patriotic feelings were with America and that Japan meant nothing. But how could that really be? Was it possible that some of my very neighbors sat in the cockpits of the warplanes that came in over our city each evening? Was it possible even that those pilot's goggles that Kazuko had seen had hidden a pair of Japanese eyes?

Milo began splashing, sitting at the edge of the tub I was in, and I remembered what Kazuko had said once, of people who emigrated as we had. She had said that real Americans were so tall and odd looking that to live among them would take an act of extraordinary courage. My people were farmers, and Kazuko had said that she could only imagine them always on the lookout for intruding Americans, living like that in a land of giants. Surely, she said, if they had farms bordered by the enemy they were always in great danger of having those farms swept away, of simply having a wide-eyed neighbor come in and claim the land as his own. She also thought that perhaps the Japanese were considered valuable as food growers or worked so well that the job of dirt farmer no longer had to be done by white men.

Milo was lying on his side, his eyes searching my face from the edge of the tub, so I stood quickly and lifted him into my arms. We went to the corner of the room and called over the wall to his mother, telling her that we would wait for her outside, and I could hear the women's voices starting up again as we stepped back into the dressing room.

Milo was happy as I dried him and slipped his clean clothes on over his head. My own *yukata* seemed too heavy and hot now, so I tied it together quickly and was about to carry Milo into the cooler foyer when I noticed a man fumbling with the knot of his obi, just inside the door of the men's section. We could hear the familiar droning, high above us, of the enemy planes, but I went over and offered to help the man with his knot. Milo smiled at him as the sound of the engines disappeared.

"Sir, let me help you," I said. "You are lucky, for the bath water is hot and you will have the place to yourself."

The man turned slowly to look at me, his age encasing him, and it took me a moment to understand that this, again, was Kazuko's old tea teacher.

"The knot of my obi has tightened itself," he said. "I always try to tie it loosely but it has a mind of its own. Several times lately I have had to cut myself out of my own kimono. An obi should encircle a man but not contain him."

The *sensei* thrust his belly forward and raised his hands so that I could get at his knot more easily.

"I have never known an obi to be so independent before," he said. "Perhaps I am contributing to its tightening by the way I walk. I lean back farther than I used to. I try to compensate for a tendency I have toward bending so far forward that my eyes always search the ground."

The knot on the teacher's obi was impossible. He peered at it along with me, his wrinkled face clearly worried about it.

"What can I do?" he asked. "All of my obi are now cut across the middle and strewn about my house, their knots still clutching at them. They remind me of those animals that will not release the awful grip of their jaws, even in death. What are those animals called? I forgot."

Though my fingers were strong, the knot was such that I could not even find an edge at which to work. "I will have to get a tool or something," I told him. "Something to insert into the knot, something with which to work it loose." I didn't know whether the teacher recognized me or not, so changed was I from the day he found me, but he called after me saying, "Don't get scissors. That is all I ask. The obi I am wearing is the last that I own. Cut it and I will not again be able to close my kimono. I would be arrested for walking the streets the way that I would."

I went back into the foyer and asked the cashier if she had something that would work for stubborn knots. But by this time Kazuko and her mother and several others were there so we all went back in, the owner of the bath leading us and carrying a small nutpick in her hands. When she looked at the teacher standing there she seemed surprised. "This is not one of our regular customers," she said. "He laid his money on the counter when I was out of the room."

"This is my wife's tea teacher," I told her, and Kazuko, looking surprised herself, gave the man a quick bow.

"I live toward Otori shrine but I have somehow extended my evening walk and now feel the need for a bath," the teacher told us.

Kazuko's mother bowed to the teacher and took the nutpick from the bath owner. "Really," she said, "a knot is a knot." The teacher bowed to the group and when Kazuko's mother came forward with the pick he thrust his abdomen out again, the knot riding on the sharp edge of his bony hip. "This always happens to me," he said.

When Kazuko's mother went to work on the knot, the rest of us came close to see what success she was having. The teacher had his elbows pointed out, his old hands turned at angles on his hips. The nutpick kissed the edges of the knot for a while, searching for a place to enter, but being careful not to pull at the threads of the material itself.

"Really," the teacher said, once or twice.

It is my opinion that Kazuko's mother would have opened the knot, though, of course, the point is academic now, for as she picked so softly the sky was full of sound. There was a roar, like a freight train coming quickly past, and then there was an explosion. We all froze in our positions there. I remember believing that as long as there was no whistle, no bomb would come sliding down its musical scale to harm us. Nevertheless, there was a terrific shaking of the earth that had been quiet for so long. I closed my eyes and waited, but the bath still stood.

"Oh," said the *sensei*. "Have you cut it? Will I be forced, from now on, to wear western clothes?"

As he spoke the electricity went out and the women around me started to cry. Through the frosted windows of the bath we could see the patient orange lapping of flames and we could quickly see each other, a little, in its light. During the awful moaning of the women, Milo began to perk up and giggle once again. His hands flapped about in the dark air and he jumped up and down beside me like a happy frog.

The women and the teacher formed a single line and, controlling panic, began to walk slowly out, with me and Milo taking up the rear. We went through the bathhouse and out the double front doors. Though the noise had been deafening, none of the stores around us seemed to have been hit and the orange glow that we'd seen through the window was considerably farther off than we'd first imagined. Though the lights had gone out it was not very dark on the street. People stood in front of their stores, some with buckets in their hands, some pulling their hair and crying. "The bath! The bath water!" they called. "We must wet down the sides of the buildings!"

It was true; the newspapers had printed a set of rules for dealing with the possibility of fire, and one of them had been to take water from the tubs of the neighborhood baths, to douse the sides of the wooden homes and buildings. The owner of the bath took a step farther forward and said, "Please. Do not worry about the softness of my tatami. Help yourselves. Please."

Buckets appeared. Neighbors, their faces dark, marched through the bath's light entrance and across the heavy tiles to the tubs. At first the water was too hot and they tried to fill their buckets too full, so there were shouts of pain. And quickly the tatami was soaked and torn, the heels of street shoes turning its straight straw lines into twisted sores, like the blooms of an awful flower.

"Help yourselves," the bath woman kept saying. "Welcome. Welcome."

There were a dozen stores on either side of the bath, on either side of the street, and all were wooden. The owner of the bath ran to the back of the building to turn off the fire that heated the water. The store owners and their families were taking the water that they got from the tubs and throwing it as high up the walls of their buildings as they could. Some of the women standing with us began to try to help, bringing the smaller bath buckets out and heaving water all around. Milo and I stood for a moment, in the middle of everything, and then we walked away, down the street toward the oranging sky.

The glow of a fire from a distance does not show the sharpness of its flames. Other people were walking the way we were but they had about them an awkward sense of cheerfulness, not angry that it was Kazuko's spider-faced enemy who'd done this, but rather seeing it as a break in the routine, as something to do in the evening. It was, after all, a neighborhood first.

The bomb had landed only two streets away and when we got to the edge of Meguro-dori, the wide boulevard that cut our section of Tokyo into halves, Kazuko and her mother caught up with us. Her mother's hand was still wrapped tightly around the *sensei's* stubborn obi and she was pulling him along, his angle of walking unchanged, his abdomen still forward. We could see the fire plainly now; it was centered in the Buddhist temple on the other side of the street. The teacher took my arm. "I know that temple," he said. "I have done tea there."

Across the street there were fire fighters positioned everywhere, but they handled the hoses poorly and did not try to keep the crowd back. We crossed quickly and entered the temple garden as casually as we had on our Sunday outing, Kazuko's mother and the *sensei* walking a few meters ahead of Kazuko, Milo, and me. There were many small fires, much of the foliage was burning, but the main building itself was being watered so that the flames on its walls might not reach the roof.

"Wooden Tokyo has always invited fire," the *sensei* said. "It is one of the dilemmas of our life-style."

Most of the others in the crowd had contented themselves with watching from the safety of the street, and as soon as we were within the temple grounds I began to wish we had done the same. I was hot and perspiring, worried that some accident might befall us. Kazuko's mother and the *sensei* had run to the center of the little bridge that spanned one of the carp ponds and were looking about like tourists, nudging each other and pointing off at parts of the spectacular destruction. By the time we caught up with them dozens of spotted carp were gathered beneath the bridge, their stupid mouths wide and hungry at the surface of the pond.

"We should go back," I said. "We are getting too close." But Kazuko's mother was on the tips of her toes, pointing to an area off the temple grounds, on the temple's far side, where we could see the sway of the flames in the rising wind.

The bridge we stood upon was one of several in the large temple yard, and, as the small fires multiplied around us, we began to lose our sense of direction. Had we stepped upon the bridge from this side or from that? The gathered carp below us looked like lepers and when a bit of fire slid into the pond on the far side they all turned to the hissing.

"Let's go," I said, but as we stepped from the bridge fire leaped from one to another of a line of ginkgo trees that stretched in front of us. Kazuko took my arm. The trees burned quickly, their orange skirts dancing brightly before falling quietly down. "Help," said the *sensei*, surprised and jumping a little. He and Kazuko's mother were both ready to leave then, but each was sure of a different direction.

We could see the great main hall in front of us, so I stopped a moment and tried to concentrate, to discover once again, in which part of the yard we stood. Small fires wandered up the sides of the big building and the smoke pouring through the roof was as thick as velvet. I looked at Milo and saw that he was lulled by the fire, the brightness of it making him hold his eyes nearly closed. I had just come to a decision as to which way we should turn when Kazuko screamed and released the grip she had on my arm. She pointed the fingers of both hands at the temple roof, making me look there just in time to see it blow. Parts of the roof rose like projectiles, and it was as if they were trying to strike back at the Americans, so high into the sky did some parts go. Individual boards turned in the air above us like stiff acrobats, their long wigs waving to the crowd. We were so close we might have been killed by their return to earth, but something in the air made them drop straight back down, landing like deadweights to push the remaining timbers in on the poor Buddha, whom we could see then, still otherworldly, through the disintegrating walls.

Kazuko moaned beside me, her fingers now pointing at the ground, her body so stiff that I thought she would fall. The *sensei* had his thumbs hooked in his obi, but stepped behind Kazuko and began shouting in her ear. "Calm yourself! Calm yourself! The fire is dying!"

Indeed, though the fire was raging, with the bulk of the temple no longer blocking our view, we could see clearly which way we had to go. We could see the patrons of the fire standing all along Meguro-dori, swaying in their summer *yukata*, and we were able to step away from the menacing trees.

With the roof missing even the firemen seemed to have given up, for there was nothing specific left for them to fight. They stood in circles, agreeing among themselves that the fire would not leap, this evening, to some unscorched portion of their shrinking city.

In a moment the *sensei* and I were able to get everyone moving again, slowly back to safety. We took the long way, giving the angry building a wide berth, but when I looked, one last time, in at the Buddha, I saw a little of the color of the fire across its forehead, a little change in its fine expression. The essence of the temple building, bits and pieces of its walls and roof, still stood, and it reminded me of a potter's kiln, so hot did it look in there. Was I mistaken or were the Buddha's lips losing some of their fine pursed quality? Was the Buddha's mouth opening slowly? To form a small circle, a look of slight surprise?

I stopped again and pointed for the others, so that they also could see their Buddha melt, but they were beyond me and had fixed their mad expressions on something more substantial. There before them, on a piece of garden where stones had recently been raked into meditative swirls, the bodies of some of the temple monks were gathered. That they were monks I understood from the remnants of cloth that had been singed to the arms and legs of some, like extra layers of thick protective skin. Kazuko's mother and the tea teacher stood quietly, their own mouths opened like the Buddha's, their hands moving slowly in the air like deaf-mutes speaking. Surely the monks could have saved themselves, I thought, by running from the fire as they'd recently run from Kazuko's mother and her plaintive shouts. Among the monks the rounder body of the temple master drew me, for he alone was still sitting up. His fat legs were forever crossed, and beside him he held, in one of his charcoal hands, the merest shell of his *shamisen*, its three strings sprung skyward then burned back down, like fuses. There were no expressions on the faces of any of the monks. The fire had given them hideous burns, their noses snipped from them, their mouths gone, no surprise at all on their uniform faces.

Kazuko put her hands to my cheeks, pulled me toward her, and whispered. "Could we go home now? If we stay longer we will lose what ability we have left to understand what is happening to us."

The firemen had turned their hoses on once again and were running high streams of water onto our Buddha, fixing his new expression for us all to see. His lips, always before so prim, appeared now to be drooling, his jaw, always before so firm, was now slightly askew. It was as if this fire had given him real life and then quickly singed his heart. It was as if he had altered his expression of his own free will.

As we turned to leave, others began streaming across Meguro-dori, for the danger of the fire was less. Around the dead monks the air seemed cooler. Behind us the burnt ginkgo trees were spent and slump-shouldered, heads hung like beggars', thin and ashamed. Kazuko's mother and the tea teacher held hands and walked slowly, and when we got to a certain street we took a shortcut, one we always used when coming from that direction. The shortcut was so nice and familiar that I regained, a little, my feeling of the permanence of things. People were sleeping here, under the cool light of the moon. When we got to our gate we waited for Kazuko's mother and the *sensei*. The night was actually mild. Across my arms Milo was quiet and smiling. He had opened his eyes again and I could see the fire still burning in them.

*

KAZUKO's *sensei* stayed at our house that night and for many nights thereafter. In the morning, when dawn crept in so normally, he told us that he'd had a bomb too, landing somewhere near his home, and that his obi knot had been pulled tight by his wandering hands as he walked the streets in search of a place to get clean. When he left his house, he told us, the flames were licking its back side, his storage shed was already gone, and the acrid smell of burning tea was in the air. "It was not unpleasant," he said. "The odor of my life was everywhere. All of the neighbors took a moment in their fleeing to put their noses to the wind and remember me."

During the next weeks the constant humming engines of the enemy planes gave Tokyo its rhythm. When our house was finally burned we were away at the bath, just as Kazuko's mother had always predicted. We had packed a few valuables, Kazuko's tea bowls, a little money, and had buried them in a safe place, under the loose earth at the foot of our fig tree, so we had more than many of the others did, should we ever get back home again. The sky was orange above our house when we left the bath but we'd lost interest in looking at fire and did not return. Instead we headed, without comment, toward where we knew government resettlement buses, sooner or later, would come to take us away.

There is little more to tell. Once we were settled outside the city we heard the sounds of American planes so often that many of us no longer even noticed. Kazuko and her mother and the *sensei* and Milo and I were given a canvas shelter and were able to stay together; that's something. We cooked rice over a small hibachi built at a central location. The entire camp was in good order. It was quiet and no one interrupted the fragile thoughts of his neighbor. Bulletins were posted everywhere, testimonials as to how we were winning the war. It was the government's way of telling us, I think, that we were lost.

No one we knew, none of our neighbors and not even the *sensei*, had ever been so far south as Hiroshima, but it was the consensus that, across the surface of the camp, there was a perceptible movement of liquids at the precise moment that the American bomb was dropped. The *sensei* was doing tea, he said, and even the thick liquid in his cup turned a bit, bubbling once, like lava. Soon after that the planes stopped coming altogether and the bulletin board remained unchanged. Everyone was so sad, so resigned to the arrival of the Americans. They were all looking forward to more pain, to violence, this time perpetrated on a one-to-one basis, eye-to-eye. But I did not think that would happen. Now that the war was over the Americans would walk our streets calmly, I knew, and we would be left alone. It was I, not the others, who understood how it would really be. Incidences of violence would be rare. Insubordination would be unheard-of, and the Americans would be surprised at that. The Japanese would be model prisoners. That had been Major Nakamura's point.

One day, after a second bomb was dropped on Nagasaki, I left the camp by myself. I took the bus into town and walked the kilometer or so necessary to find that untouchable street, to find Meguro-dori, to see where we had lived. As I walked I got lost, for the landmarks I'd always recognized were gone. In a few places buildings stood as if whole, in others only the tops were missing, but if I walked into what used to be their centers I still found myself outside of things. As I got closer to where we had lived, the rubble and clutter grew, the presence of people diminished. I was wearing, stupidly, my only remaining pair of American pants, and I was busy, most of the time, brushing the soot from them, trying to step high to keep my canvas shoes clean.

Everything I saw reminded me of a forest fire I'd seen once, from the window of a train, as we'd slowly passed through the mountains of northern California. Buildings were stumps, streets were charred earth, schools and marketplaces were roughly burned fields. Perhaps because I wore such odd clothes I felt onstage and acted up a bit at the approximate location of our old house. As I stepped high and turned in the surprising wind I came to the spot where Kazuko had hidden her beautiful bowls, and I found one of them, untouched by the fire. The leaves of the fig tree above the bowl were rolled tightly and still hung, most of them, like charred cigars, from the branches of the dead tree. I stopped moving then and dug, with my fingers, to see what else I could find under the earth. Our money was there, and a paper bag containing photographs. A few feet away, where our sleeping room had been, I saw the little feet of my calico cat, and that stopped me from searching further. The cat looked like a small version of the monks we had seen and I was nearly sick. Though I had been strong through human death and misery I could not face the roasted body of my cat. I retched once against the side of the fig tree and then stumbled clumsily away from there. I thought, even a charmed life then, even a life which appears to be protected by something outside what we call luck, can find a place in the ashes at any time. There is always room for it among the ruins.

The end of the war came out of a quiet sky. People in the camps and on the street were increasingly nervous, increasingly willing to chatter. Though the sky had been silent for days there were still no Japanese soldiers home, except for the few who had been there as long as I had, the ones with the missing parts, some of whom already sat at the dirt edges of the camps, tin cups placed where their laps had once been.

Each day seemed exactly like the one before it, exactly like the next, but finally, as we were milling about, walking in aimless circles and nodding to those we passed, the camp commander got on the loudspeaker and told us that the next voice we heard would be that of the Emperor. We all laughed in disbelief and kicked the dirt about us gently with the toes of our shoes. But a voice did come to us, all sad and sounding, suspiciously, like the camp administrator himself. It was a high-pitched voice and, though it was almost impossible to understand, there was something in it that reminded me of my father the farmer, dead to me for so long.

> To our good and loyal subjects: After pondering deeply the general trends of the world and the actual conditions obtaining in our empire today, we have decided to effect a settlement of the present situation by resorting to an extraordinary measure.

What? Surely if that was the Emperor speaking, the extraordinary measure was that he was doing so.

> We have ordered our government to communicate to the governments of the United States, Great Britain, China, and the Soviet Union that our empire accepts the provisions of their joint declaration.
> To strive for the common prosperity and happiness of all nations as well as the security and well-being of our subjects is the solemn obligation which has been handed down by our imperial ancestry and which we lay close to the heart.
> Indeed, we declared war on America and Britain out of our sincere desire to insure Japan's self-preservation and the stabilization of East Asia, it being far from our thoughts either to infringe upon the sovereignty of other nations or to embark upon territorial aggrandizement. . . .

Certainly not! It was the Americans who were infringing upon Japan, with bombs! Territorial aggrandizement with bombs and with fire!

> . . . The enemy has begun to employ a new and most cruel bomb, the power of which to do damage is, indeed, incalculable, taking the toll of many innocent lives. Should

we continue to fight, it would not only result in an ultimate collapse and obliteration of the Japanese nation, but also it would lead to the total extinction of human civilization.

This was not the Emperor speaking, but some politician in his place. The people around me all listened with their heads bowed. Could it be that they were taken in?

We are keenly aware of the inmost feelings of all of you, our subjects. However, it is according to the dictates of time and fate that we have resolved to pave the way for a grand and lasting peace for all the generations to come by enduring the unavoidable and suffering what is unsufferable. Having been able to save and maintain the structure of the Imperial State, we are always with you, our good and loyal subjects, relying upon your sincerity and integrity.

Beware most strictly of any outbursts of emotion that may engender needless complications, of any fraternal contention and strife that may create confusion, lead you astray, and cause you to lose the confidence of the world.

Who was this man who spoke to us? He had not been inside these camps, that was clear. There were no outbursts here, would never be.

Let the entire nation continue as one family from generation to generation, ever firm in its faith of the imperishableness of its divine land, and mindful of its heavy burden of responsibilities, and the long road before it. Unite your total strength to be devoted to the construction for the future. Cultivate the ways of rectitude, nobility of spirit, and work with resolution so that you may enhance the innate glory of the Imperial State and keep pace with the progress of the world.

The loudspeaker crackled as it always did when the camp commander wanted us to know that an announcement was over.

"Who was that really?" the tea teacher asked, and I found myself saying, "That was he. No question about it."

It was the last blow needed to bring us to our knees. Large tracts of burn had scarred the city, Hiroshima and Nagasaki were gone, but it was the Emperor's speech that made us want to weep. Jimmy and Ike were dead. My son was woefully attracted to the scars that the fires had left, loved the look of destruction across the earth, was already showing signs of the oddness of his other father. Kazuko and her mother and her tea teacher stood beside me there in the relocation camp and what they felt, what I could see across their faces, was shame. It was over. The war was over. The bodies of the Buddhist monks could not withstand the lick of the flames any better than mine would have, but I had survived while most of the people I had known were dead, most of the remainder lost to me. Our losses were incalculable but it was interesting, I think, that though whole cities had been taken from us we were crying then for our most important loss. The virginity of the Emperor's voice.

*

THOSE days and the days following were very bad for the Japanese. All around the war zone officers sat naked to their waists, the sharp points of ritual swords pressed tightly against their bellies. Their intestines came upon the world with an ironic kind of robust energy, all healthy-looking next to them on the failed ground. In Tokyo there was little impulse to die but there was chaos. There were only tents, and cardboard covers that people held around themselves when it rained.

After the war I put off, for a while, my search for the American officials who could give me safe passage back to the longed-for life of Los Angeles. After the war I could do nothing but lie about listening to General MacArthur telling us to forsake, forever, our wayward ways, to look toward peaceful means, toward trade and textiles. He said that he believed in Japan and that America would someday learn to forgive and forget. "Let it be in the market-place that you once more work your way to the top," he said.

I can remember very well MacArthur's English speeches and the obscure, meaningless, translations given them by his aides. And the more I heard from MacArthur, the more he spoke, the surer I was that I would not be forgiven, that I would be among those for whom the great general would not be able to find room in his vast and wonderful heart. His megalomania would be my downfall, I feared, and in my small room, with cardboard all around me I realized the irony of my fate. Toward the middle of that year the radio began to introduce MacArthur's speeches with music, you see, and the tune that they found to play was my rendition of "Mood Indigo," from a recording never re-leased, Ike's best work on behalf of Jimmy's poor old band.

"*You ain't been blue,*" I sang, just before MacArthur came on with his somber tones, his gift of guilt. "*You ain't been blue. No . . . No . . . No . . . You ain't been blue . . . 'Til you've had that mood indigo. . . .*" He wanted us unhappy in shades of the rainbow the Japanese could not even recog-nize. Yet the people loved him and it was not long until that tune, my tune, was heard everywhere in the rebuilding city. And when finally I came forward, as I knew I must, I was swept to fame by it. I had the first hit song of postwar Japan and when it was released to the general public it bore the name Teddy Maki, with no sign of the AyJays, no sign of Jimmy Yamamoto at all.

By the time the Korean war started I was the best-known entertainer in all of Japan. I began to mix my American tunes with those of the new composers, and I took Milo before the cameras so the people watching could see him grow, so that he could become their darling. I lost my American citizenship and Milo grew away from me and Kazuko became the wife that I have so often cheated in the sharing of my evening time. I have had Sachiko and I have had my little tricks, the ones I like to play on Americans, if I can find them, at train and subway stations. For a man whose early life took such odd turns my present one is very staid. If, internally, my chaos has continued, on the outside all seems serene and sequential, I am sure.

The Korean war brought MacArthur back to the front for a while. The Japanese people, in their fervor to be forgiven, to make up for all that they had done, tried to take the general's good advice to heart. There was a presidential election coming up and MacArthur, with the settlement of Japan under his belt, let his broad-billed cap cast its shadow, for a while, over the semblance of a candidacy. It was clear that all of Japan supported him. I was well into my coasting period, well into the time when I did not think of my past at all, when the government of Tokyo posted a sign high across a stretch of street in Ginza, the busiest section of town. *We Play for MacArthur's Erection!* the sign said, and as I look back on it I realize that it spawned in me the embryo of my present life. *We Play for MacArthur's Erection!* Soon those transposed consonants were corrected but the truth of it was not lost on me. On the "Amateur Hour" my own small campaign was ignited by them. As the show's popularity grew I made sure that its taste and quality diminished. Surely, I thought, I will find a level of entertainment so low that it will defeat even Japan's appetite for the awful, the insipid, the mundane. But though I have tried, that level is still not found. "Mood Indigo" greets the nation each week so ironically, and the whole idea has made me rich. I am living in a country of farters and contortionists, a world as full of them as Arabia is of oil. Plasticity can control Japan as it has America, I have faith, though Japan is the last real holdout of the modern world.

*

PART TWO

I MUST have dozed in the back seat of the cab for when I awoke the taxi driver was grumbling, anxious to get home himself, to drop me in the low street though I knew immediately that Sachiko had not returned. I let myself into her room with my latchkey. This room is Sachiko's personal domain, one that I should not have been in alone, but the coldness of the night precluded my waiting outside. Before entering the room I walked all around the building but the air was even cooler than in Roppongi and the alley behind the building was too narrow to traverse with ease. When I looked up I could not make out her room. I could see the moon, though, which showed me some debris along the path.

Have I mentioned that twice in the nineteen-fifties and once in the sixties I was voted Entertainer of the Year? My mind was on it then, my whole being aimed at it. Kazuko and I were happy, we were sane and quiet with each other, at least, and we made strides. All during those years, more than thirty of them, we were involved with accumulation. Kazuko maintained a sense of order about our lives while I moved up and down on the popularity polls. And though as a girl Kazuko had been interested in western things, as we grew older she began to change. As if to honor her mother she started wearing kimonos much of the time. Indeed, after her mother's death she made her mother's closet her own, her mother's wardrobe her preferred attire. Yet unlike her mother's, Kazuko's was not the voice of criticism but that of consideration, of high regard. She has never mentioned the past, not once, after Milo's birth, mentioned his other father. And if Kazuko and I do not speak often, at least we speak well, our conversation free of platitudes. About Kazuko I can say that ever since I became her husband she has been my wife. It is not so much that she loves me, you understand, but that she is simply of me, a part of the whole. It isn't happiness which Kazuko chases but a sense of rhythm, a motion that flows with the rest of her world.

Why then, it must be asked, have I come, alone, to the empty room of my mistress? Surely I knew that she was hiding, waiting within the dark confines of the bar for my passing. Why could I not have stayed with my son or ridden home safely in his limousine? The answer is that some time ago, from below the placid surface of my middle age, I began to anticipate a change. At first it was a remembrance, the floating up of random visions of war, but later it took on more concrete tones. Occasionally I would wake, after initially sleeping soundly, only to find myself unable to return to sleep. And my dreams began to take on a certain cadence. In one, which recurred, I was a small boy hiding in an apple crate at the side of the road. I had a hammer with me in the crate and I would reach out and pound the hammer down upon the toes of passing soldiers, wounding them all. I was terrified that they would catch me but I kept my hammer moving just the same. And yet, as I have said, all during that time I was not an unhappy man. I knew my show was poor but I had not focused, greatly, upon why I wanted it so. And misleading Americans was a mere hobby. No, my real life, up until the time I met Sachiko, was simply this: I worked, I saw my son, I went home to my wife and the accumulations which surrounded us.

In the beginning Sachiko was just another bar girl in a bar I frequented with my colleagues. She was likable because she was not a talker but aside from that I had not taken any special notice of her. And then one evening she mentioned to me that she was from Hiroshima. When she said it I was struck with a curiosity to know more and when I asked if she had been hurt by the bomb she pulled the sleeves of her kimono back and showed me the beginnings of her scars. How, I asked, had it felt? How clearly, I wanted to know, did she remember it? Her calmness and demure answers only served to awaken in me a deeper urge to see all of what the bomb had done to her body. And soon the soldiers in my dreams gave way to a vision of the war opening up over her city. I saw her running. I heard her cry. I was still awakened in the night, but now, while Kazuko slept so neatly beside me, I began imagining what a sight the girl's body might be. And slowly it became a compulsion. I felt that I was about to take a step that had awaited me in time and that was inevitable. It was the beginning of a thaw, a moment when the distant events of my youth were about to forgo their dormancy. And Sachiko, somehow, was to be the key. Soon I began to pester her, to wait at the bar until everyone else had left, and to make propositions. Sachiko told me, finally, that she would consider the possibility of a liaison, but never that of a one-night stand. So after more than three decades of my knowing only Kazuko, Sachiko and I left the bar one night and made our way to her room. Like all bar girls Sachiko was in need of a sponsor in order to strike out on her own and I had said I would look into this bar called the Kado, one that she had informed me was for sale.

When Sachiko brought me home that first night it was not, of course, to talk business, not to go into the terms of our agreement nor to discuss the kind of clientele the Kado would have. What Sachiko had in mind was the consummation. She took my coat and hung it, an intruder among her gowns. She offered me tea and then sweetly (she was always generous in her business dealings) removed her clothes.

I am sure that Sachiko's scars would not have seemed unpleasant to another man, but when I touched them that first night I was moved in a peculiar way. It was as if the air in the room held some special gas, some drug with an imperceptibly light touch. I let my hand rest across her middle, not my whole hand, really, but the tips of my five fingers. The surface of her scar gave a little, was not as tight as it looked, not as thick. And though to my eye it was a crust with spurs and sores randomly spotting it, to my hand it was a delicate thing. Sachiko backed away and I could tell by her movement that what I felt she did not feel correspondingly. She did not know whether they touched or not, her wound and those five fingertips of mine.

For a long time we stood that way but finally Sachiko lay down on her bed while I sat cross-legged beside her, gazing into the pattern that her scars made and deciding what to do. I had been obsessed by the girl, obsessed to the point of agreeing to finance a business for her, yet as she cheerfully prepared to fulfill her end of our bargain I was all aquiver, all reticence and cold-handed with nerves. I wanted to tell her that I was American and that it was the war that joined us but she knew the former and the latter would have left us feeling strange. It was not, after all, her body that I wanted but her closeness, my hands upon her scars, an absence of clothing between us.

As I look back on it from this distance of nearly three years I realize that Sachiko was a kind girl. I must have looked scandalous, my gooseflesh rising, my chest cavity heaving, my desire so different from her own. Yet all during our time together she never laughed her easy laugh at me.

She never, until recently, denied her presence when I knocked so bravely on the Kado's hard door. Ours was a liaison made of wounds, though hers she wore freely while mine hung like pendants from my old thin neck.

Have I said it clearly enough? Until I met Sachiko I had been like a man on a rotisserie turning evenly but thoughtlessly through time. Yet when Sachiko told me of her birthplace, when I placed my hands upon her scars and sat staring into them, I felt the crystals of some internal hourglass begin to drain. I *knew* something was about to take place that would let me continue my real life to its conclusion. And that is what I am about to tell. Just as Sachiko tired of my fingers on her wounds, my hourglass ran out, my period of waiting was over. I stayed the entire night on Sachiko's bed in a state of wakeful rest. I see now that I was preparing myself. In the morning I walked toward the events I am about to describe easily and with calm.

*

THE cold December morning made me feel, for a while, as though I had had a good night's sleep. When I left Sachiko's room it was very early, yet late enough for light to have swept across the empty streets. It was Sunday and to my surprise it had snowed during the night. Though I had been awake I had not heard the snowflakes fall and as I walked toward a larger street I imagined them landing, one atop the other, in their slow descent. It was as if everything had been prepared as a surprise for me. The marks my shoes made were the only blemish on the fresh new day.

I was beginning to feel a lightness of heart, beginning to realize once again that often the thoughts a man has at night cannot be supported during the optimistic hours of day, when I arrived home to find my entire family outside, standing in front of our house and pacing about with frowns on their faces. Kazuko was stern-looking at the gate and for a moment I thought I was in America and that she was angry at my late arrival. My son's big car was there with Milo holding his mother's elbow and Junichi nervously standing behind him. I thought quickly that someone must have died, but the ancient *sensei* (Yes, he is still alive!) was sitting on a canvas folding chair, a director's chair that I had given him and that he liked to have with him if he went too far from the house. There was no one else whose death could cause such posturing. Had the house burned? Had someone been arrested? They all stood around in overcoats, oblivious to the snow. Milo saw me coming and ran my way.

"Father," he said, "it is my uncle. He is coming home."

But Milo had no uncles. My brothers in America knew nothing of me, could not be coming here. They were dead or lost to us. I looked at Kazuko, but Milo spoke again. "It's true," he said. "I got his photo out to remind you of what he looked like."

Milo was jumping around in front of me so spastically that I could not get a look, past him, at his mother's face. It was clear, though, that he was trying to contain himself as he held a silver-framed photograph before my eyes. Ike. It was Ike. It was Kazuko's brother Ike.

"Ike is dead," I said calmly. "I've told you the story. I was there when it happened."

"We received a call," said Milo. "If you had been any later we'd have left without you."

Gradually it came to me then that my son was serious. He was telling me that Kazuko's brother was alive and that he was coming home, would be home that day. I felt, as I stood there staring at all of them, a tingling sensation at the back of my neck. It was a slightly painful, not very pleasant, feeling, like the revitalization of a foot after an hour's dead sleep. This was not what I had expected. I had assumed that any change in my life would come about internally.

"Don't worry," I said, addressing Kazuko past my son's anxious face. "Ike is dead. I'm sure of it."

But Milo was talking again, was in mid-sentence before I began to listen to what he said. ". . . it came sometime late last night," he told me. "For some reason there was no advance notice at all. We've got to go. It was all I could do to keep them from sending a government car to get us."

Milo's chauffeur, listening more carefully than any of the rest of us, had the *sensei* in the car and was guiding Kazuko and me toward the back seat before I could protest. The young photograph of Ike was still before my eyes though Milo had already tucked it inside his jacket.

"There is some mistake," I told them. "Ike was killed very early in the war. He had been disappointed in life and wished it upon himself."

I looked at Kazuko but she wasn't listening to me. I saw a sternness across her eyes, a certain resolve across her mouth and chin. When last she'd seen her brother she'd been young and pretty and I wondered if she was worried about what he would think of her now. If Ike were truly alive I imagined that the jungle had left him tough and ageless while the rest of us had grown soft in ordinary time. But surely, if he was alive, he had known that the war was over. What was all the commotion about? He could have walked out anytime and been sent home a hero.

The four of us sat in the back seat, with loyal Junichi in the front alone. As we rode onto the expressway the tea teacher reached over and took my hand. He was looking out across the rows of busy factories and I wondered if what he saw there was rice. Even I could remember when such long billboards had not streaked the horizon. So what would Ike make of it all? In the stories I'd told of him I'd always pictured a young Ike lying still and lifeless among the jungle leaves. I imagined insects living in him as if he'd been dead only hours. And I had never portrayed him as a conventional man. He had been a jazz fan, a road manager for my band. Why then would he, of all soldiers, if he was truly alive, have stayed for so many years in that distant jungle, away from artificial sound?

The tea teacher let go of my hand and laughed, bringing everybody out of themselves. "I was nearly sixty when the war began," he said. "They wouldn't have taken me even if I'd volunteered." He leaned up and poked Junichi on the shoulder. "I fought, mind you, but not in that war. I fought against the Russians, who were extremely tough. We beat them but lost to the Americans. That's the way it was but now it seems as though things should have been reversed."

Junichi smiled at him so the *sensei* kept talking, relieving, for the rest of us, some of the tension of the growing silence. I could tell that among us only my son was not thinking about his uncle for he was looking out the window and bouncing his knee in time with some internal song, some piece of popular music floating through his brain. How had he gotten the news of Ike so early? Kazuko's message must have awaited him upon his return from the bars.

"Look!" Kazuko said. "Airplanes are circling. Will my brother be in one of those? Will he arrive first or will we?" Kazuko was all sisterly in the way she tucked the folds of her kimono into the tight band of her obi and when I rolled down my window I could see an airplane coming low out of the southern sky. Indeed, like returning bombers, there were several other airplanes moving around above us. So much had changed since the war. It was impossible that Ike could be alive. Whoever had started the story had perpetrated a cruel hoax. How long, I wondered, would it take us to get back to normal?

When we stopped in front of the international arrival section there were newspapermen and there was television. I got out of the car first and the crowd parted to allow my entry to the building. I could not help imagining Ike sitting above us somewhere, perhaps trying to make small talk with the person next to him. I wondered, had he spoken during the last thirty years? Did he have friends in the jungle? People he was leaving behind?

The television crew was made up of men that Milo knew and one of them asked him if he and I would do an interview before the plane arrived. I had gone immediately to the desk of the airline and when they entered the building was checking on the time of the flight, checking the passenger manifest to see if I could find Ike's name. Milo walked up behind me on little cat's feet.

"They'd like a word with us," he said. "One of the crews from the station."

"No," I answered.

Well, the crew had followed Milo to the desk so there was no getting out of it, nothing I could do. They had turned on their lights and we were live, the nation was catching me turning around.

"It is incredible," said the announcer, "that this latest of wartime stragglers should be of the Maki family, so much in the entertainment news these days."

I looked at Milo in a disgusted way, but put a slight smile on my face and said, "He's not of the Maki family, really, but of a family of his own."

I saw myself in the monitor and as I was speaking I looked very tired, as if it were I who had just returned from the war. The reporter turned the microphone to my son.

"Milo Maki?" he asked.

"I've never known the man," Milo told him. He frowned in his public way and tried to brush the hair from his eyes. But though the cameras were running it was clear that Milo could think of nothing more to say. When the pause grew too long the announcer began speaking, describing the scene at the airport, the government people, the family. And while he spoke the tea teacher came up behind him. Junichi and a member of the television crew stood with him, one to each side. The lights were bright in his eyes.

"Here's a man," one of the crew members whispered to the announcer. "Lives with the Makis, remembers everything."

The television announcer turned toward them and then back to his audience. Milo and I were still standing at his side but in a moment our images were replaced by that of the teacher on the monitor.

"After all, Milo," I said. "Don't you think I have things to think about now? Why did you have to put me on TV?" But even in my obvious dismay it was a reproach much unlike anything I would have said in the past. I could not muster the energy for it. I had not slept, my neck was hurting, and I was worried about what the plane might bring.

The announcer was baffled by the quick presence of an old man on the tiny screen, but the teacher could see himself and was excited. "Teddy and Milo are on television all the time," he said. "This is a first for me."

"Did you know the man who is about to come back after all these years?" he was asked. "Do you remember him?"

"Either I don't remember him or he came to my house a time or two," the teacher said. "He may have come to fetch his sister home."

The teacher smoothed the edges of his kimono and continued. "Whether I knew him or not isn't the point, though. This man's return should make us pause in our daily affairs to reflect upon what we have become."

The airport crowd, which held a carnival air, hardly noticed the element of seriousness introduced by the old man. My brother-in-law's plane was due any moment. People were getting ready to cheer.

"Do you think the returning soldier will find Tokyo changed beyond recognition?" asked the announcer.

"He will find it so on the surface," said the teacher. "But if he'd come back immediately after the fighting he'd have found it even more changed. Remember? Everything was knocked to the ground by the bombs."

The announcer and the cameraman were both about Milo's age, younger than the aging memory of war. Junichi, who'd helped put the teacher on the air, still stood beside him and glared into the camera himself. The confusion of airport waiting had died down some.

"Have you been living with the Makis for a long time?" the announcer asked.

"Since the war," said the teacher. "Since about the time this returning man died. Every time a soldier returns we tell ourselves that there can be no more, that this one must be the last. Personally, I wouldn't be surprised to see them all come back, one at a time, out of the jungles."

The *sensei* was having such a fine time that it was a shame to have him cut off as abruptly as he was. But just as he spoke the airline announced that the flight had arrived and all cameras switched immediately to the runway. We could see the cool smiles of some official greeters; we saw the wet surface of the runway with the airliner's wheels upon it. The *sensei* looked at me and shrugged.

When we left the building Kazuko and I, bent to the winter breeze, walked before the teacher and my son. There were police cars around an area cordoned off by rope and there was more commotion, more activity over this thing, than I had expected. I watched the changing expressions on Kazuko's face, watched the seriousness of Milo. Such a short time had passed between our gaining knowledge of Ike's existence and his return. How had all these people found out about it? Was this the natural airport crowd on a Sunday morning?

We got to the arrival zone just as the plane came to a steady stop and its wheels were blocked. It took a few more moments for the workmen to push a staircase up to the opening door, but once everything was secure the door was braced and all of the other passengers were brought off first. Most of them were Japanese or Filipino businessmen, and some were reluctant to move too far away from the airplane after they'd got their feet on the ground. "What's up?" we could hear them asking each other.

When everyone else was off the plane the pilot gave us a sign and an odd-looking man walked over to the foot of the stairs. He was wearing an old soldier's uniform and I suddenly found myself wishing that all of this was not happening. The man carried a boxy hat in his hands and had, on a small shaft, an old Japanese battle flag. The pain I had been bothered by moved quickly out of my neck and down my arms. It was Nakamura! The man standing there was Major Nakamura himself! A television announcer waiting near us confirmed it for me. He was a retired elementary school principal, a pharmacist named Nakamura. It was he who had given the order which kept Ike bottled up all those years.

Kazuko took the *sensei's* arm and the *sensei* took mine. The mayor of Tokyo was there, standing just next to us, and when he gave a little nod Nakamura went slowly up the steps and disappeared into the cabin of the plane. We could see the faces of the crew in the windows of the cockpit, but Ike, if he was truly alive, was alone in the body of the aircraft, waiting for his commanding officer. Everyone became extraordinarily quiet, as if listening, trying to hear what was being said on the inside. Who knew what the man had been through? Probably he was afraid and this old commander of his was coaxing him, telling him that everything would be fine.

After ten minutes had passed those of us down below

began having a little trouble maintaining ourselves. The sight of Nakamura had undone me as much as the news of Ike, yet I could not concentrate. I was in pain and was getting cold. Was I having an attack of some kind? The *sensei*, as if directing everything, was sitting in his canvas chair again, and I wanted to ask him for it, to sit down myself.

When Nakamura finally did reappear I expected him to have another man wearing another old uniform by his side, but I was wrong. Nakamura was followed by a man who was heavy, not gaunt. The man was dressed in a fine Filipino shirt and was followed by a woman and by three pretty children, all of them wearing the same stylish clothes. Was this Ike? If so, he'd been darkened by the sun until he no longer looked Japanese at all. He didn't have a sword to surrender as one of the other returnees had had. Rather he carried two large coconuts. He smiled and held the coconuts high above him when he saw the crowd that had gathered. The tea teacher poked me in the ribs with his finger and sat up straight. "Surely this is the beginning of a new trend," he said.

The crowd had been ready to applaud but when they saw this man coming down the stairs they all stood still. His robustness, his clothes, and his obvious well-being, made the major standing next to him look old and silly. The woman and children stayed close to the man, looking out at us with a little fear. And when they got to the dignitaries who stood at the bottom of the stairs, he, Ike, peered boldly into each face, giving one of the coconuts to the most important-looking of the group. For the first time in hours I felt the need to smile, but Kazuko began to tremble at my side and I could see that, as yet, none of the irony of the way her brother looked had hit her. In a moment she stepped forward, placing herself directly in his view.

"You are my brother," she told him. "My name is Kazuko. Do you remember me?"

The man looked at Kazuko carefully, but kept his remaining coconut between them.

"Mother and grandfather are dead," Kazuko said. "Jimmy is dead too. Teddy Maki and I are married now. We have a little boy named Milo."

Ike frowned, I thought, when Kazuko mentioned me. He looked back at Nakamura and forward into the crowd. Finally I raised my hand a little, catching his eye, and for a moment he lost some of his robust tropicalness. When I stepped forward the tea teacher and Milo did too.

"Hello, Ike," I said.

"I thought you were dead," said my wife's brother.

The official government greeters smiled at this exchange, but quickly called us to a set of standing microphones when it occurred to them that there would be no nationally televised embrace. Everyone was in shock. The mayor of Tokyo spoke, but so briefly that I missed what he said entirely until he looked at Ike and asked, "Would you like to say something? All of Tokyo welcomes you home."

Ike was standing between Kazuko and me but when he realized that the mayor was talking to him he stepped right up to the microphone. The coconut that he carried made him look like a foreign dignitary, an ambassador, an emissary of some kind.

"No, thank you," he said, slowly and clearly. "Though thank you very much for asking."

Among the dignitaries was another recently returned soldier and I realized that what the television company had hoped for was a kind of panel discussion, an instant exchange of views between these two men. But though Ike smiled at the mayor he would not talk and soon the television commentators resorted to interviewing people from the general public, asking randomly for opinions. I don't know about the others out it was clear to me, even in my weakened condition, that Ike's appearance was really too surprising. If this was truly Ike, what had he been doing down there? What had been going on? I saw Milo's black car edging its way toward us and when I pointed it out to the mayor he was relieved to be able to order the way cleared so that Junichi could come to our rescue. The mayor was waving his hands around above everyone. Good old Junichi, I felt like saying.

When it finally became apparent that there would be no more ceremony, a large group of reporters surged from behind the restraining ropes, their hands and voices raised. But Junichi was too quick for them. He opened the doors from the inside and we were able to slide into the car, locking the doors before the reporters had a chance to ask even one question. It was crowded in there, with the unexpected addition of the woman and children, but we managed. Ike's unhappy wife was forced to sit on my lap, and the *sensei* kept grabbing at the children, pushing them closer and closer in around their father. I couldn't see much of anything, but I could feel, from Junichi's acceleration, that we had passed through the gate and were on the road outside. Kazuko began sobbing quietly next to me. Her brother's coconut was in her lap and was changing color in spots as her tears hit it. Everyone tried to adjust themselves for comfort. My body was betraying me but I was glad, for the moment, to be sitting down. Soon we were joined by a police escort and traffic was stopped, leaving the reporters even farther behind.

This was very ironic! Here we were, riding in from the airport, a whole foreign family on our laps! I could see Ike's wife's face by then and it wasn't happy. She kept her eyes on her husband and was trying, unsuccessfully, to keep at least part of her weight off my thin legs. Several times I thought I would speak, since the silence was becoming unbearable, but it was my son's new uncle who finally broke the ice. I could see him clearly after the shifting of bodies. He leaned forward and lit a cigarette, a roll or two of belly riding up over his tightly buckled belt. He spoke in a language I didn't understand and then said in Japanese, "Teddy Maki and I were in a fierce battle in the middle of the jungle in the middle of the night. We were being fired upon from above. Guerrillas were hiding in the trees, so we all dove for the underbrush and began shooting back."

"I thought you were dead then," said my voice, but Ike waved his hand.

"I stayed where I was, digging myself into the dirt, all night long. When daylight came I could hear the guerrillas walking over me, firing occasionally into the immobile bodies that they found. I thought Teddy Maki was among them. I am here today because I chose not to return their fire. I dug as far down into the earth as I could, that's all."

When he spoke of immobile bodies I tried to shift mine, but the woman on top of me would have none of it. She was pretending I wasn't there.

"I thought you were dead when the firing stopped," I said.

"I waited in the ground until I could hear nothing of the guerrillas and until darkness fell once more," said Ike. "I remember it was very difficult to get back out of the ground and I had the ironic thought that I would die by my own quick hands, that I would not be able to free myself from the vines and foliage above. When I was able to stand, however, I didn't know which way to turn, didn't know which way was back or which way the guerrillas had gone. I found bodies, but they had been stripped of their weapons and rations. I was afraid to cry over them for fear that the sound would bring the enemy back. So I simply walked away from the scene of the battle without having fired a shot. I stayed in the jungle for nearly six years after that. I'm not proud of it, but I wanted to tell you the truth."

If I had not been so uncomfortable, so out of sorts, I might have laughed. But while her brother had been speaking, Kazuko had been crying, and both of my legs were hurting from the weight of the woman. The tea teacher seemed happy enough to have two of the children on his lap, though. His voice came from somewhere to my right asking, "What happened next? What happened during the six years? What happened after?"

"I had no idea," said Ike, "that so much time had passed. I found a cave to live in and I camped, often, at the edges of villages, so that I could go in at night to hunt chickens, to lift garden vegetables from the soil. For months I tried to keep track of time by counting, but soon everything ran together. I would find myself standing on a path somewhere, not knowing whether one night or two had passed since last I stood there. I became accustomed to the sound and shape of the jungle but I rarely saw the moon—the canopy above was as thick as the soil beneath.

"For the first months I kept a vow of total silence, never uttering a syllable, never forgetting how I had come to be there. But later it became my purpose to lurk at the outskirts of the villages, often crouching at the backs of huts, listening to families speaking to each other. I memorized intonations, replaced my dormant Japanese grammar with bits of their own. And by the time I had sense and security enough to come out of the jungle and into their midst I had stolen clothes and had learned a few words and phrases, enough of their language for me to fool them, if I was careful, into thinking that I was a simple man from somewhere nearby."

Well, I thought, if he'd taken a total vow of silence in the jungle he was certainly making up for it now. I couldn't see Junichi but I could tell from the way the car slowed that he was lost in the story. It was just the kind of thing that he would find fascinating. Milo's new uncle took a breath and continued.

"I stayed in the village for a short time, working for pennies, slaughtering and cleaning hogs. I saved my money, slipping back into the jungle at night to eat what was free and to rethink my strategy. When I had enough saved for bus fare, when I had enough for a few days' lodging, I waved good-bye to my employer and boarded a bus for Manila. And once there I immediately found a job. A small theater near where the bus stopped was in need of a janitor. When I saw the advertisement I began to remember my days as manager of a jazz band and wondered if entertainment there would be anything like it had been in Japan. And after that things just happened naturally. From working as a janitor I got to know actors and soon I began to act and soon after that I began to teach the acting methods I had perfected while developing my disguise as a Filipino. In truth I may never have returned to Japan, but I fell ill and even a fine actor cannot fight disease. When I was sick, they tell me, I did nothing but shout and rant, all in Japanese. My wife and children prayed so hard for my survival that when they heard my strange babbling they thought I was speaking in tongues. But when they sent for the priest the priest said, 'Wait a minute.' He had had some wartime experiences of his own, I guess, and recognized the language for what it was. And so I was found out. My wife was angry for weeks after my recovery but my children took it with a shrug. 'Daddy's Japanese,' they told each other. I could hear them practicing saying it in the hallway outside my sickroom. 'Daddy's Japanese.' There are only so many ways to say that, you know. If you don't believe me try it sometime. Acting is hard. Vocal range is everything."

I laughed once and Ike reached over and put his hand on the cheek of the woman on my lap. The woman held back.

She pushed a wisp of hair from her face, but she held back, and I could tell quickly that she was far from being adjusted to the idea that all these years she had been married to a Japanese, no matter what her husband said.

"Anyway it took me a while to convince my wife that what I did was in no way intended as a ruse against her. Many sections of the Filipino population are still strict in their hatred of Japan. Yet after she found out she insisted that she had known all along. Something about the way I walked, she told me. Something about the way I brought food to my mouth.

"You know," said Ike, "when those other two lost soldiers came back to Japan before me I read about them in the Manila papers and shared in many discussions about what fools they had been. My friends and I laughed at them. We looked closely at groups of Japanese tourists with their cameras and flags. 'Could these be the same people who once so easily conquered us?' we asked each other. I wonder what my friends thought when they read about me."

I was about to respond, to say something nice to him, when Junichi did something unprecedented. He turned halfway around in his seat and spoke. "I am sure it made them think twice about the nature of Japanese people," he said. His voice was clear and strong but deeper than it was in private, and I suspected that he was lowering it to try to impress my brother-in-law. The car didn't waver on the road when he spoke, but for the first time my resolve did, my ability to view the situation lightly. Where was I to find a constant if not in Junichi's demeanor?

"Well," said Ike, "I don't know why those others stayed away as long as they did, but for me it was accidental." He swept his hands around the car at the tinted windows, but I knew what he meant. "My first and clearest memory," he said, "was that of burying myself in the foliage of the jungle and weeping. I am sure the guerrillas who hunted me could hear my sobs. But sound, in the jungle, is odd. It is not always possible to discern the direction from which it comes."

Ike put his hand on Kazuko's shoulder. "And when I came out of the jungle I was at my wits' end," he said. "I could not have gone on. When I tell the story now I make it sound easy, but it was not. The villagers nearby built a superstition around me. Because they had heard my wails coming across the trees they called me the sobbing ghost, the night crier. Once, for a short time, some of them built a small altar where they would leave food and spare pieces of clothing. I don't think they ever knew I was Japanese. They thought I was touched and they felt that if they took some slight care of me, the fine fortune and good crops of the previous years would continue. Sometimes they caught glimpses of me, I am sure, but they never gave chase. It would have been so easy for them to catch me if they had."

Junichi had been driving slowly, but he had apparently timed it just right, because just as this man finished his story we turned off the main road and stopped in front of our house. The car was quiet, everyone either lost in some corner of the story or too uncomfortable to speak.

"Is this the spot where the old house was?" Ike asked his sister when we finally did move ourselves out of the car. When he spoke to her he put his hand under her chin and turned her face so that he could see her better, and I didn't like that. Nevertheless I stepped carefully over to his wife and said, "I am your husband's brother-in-law. My name is Teddy." But the poor woman only nodded, and I could see in her eyes some of the same discomfort I felt, so I moved away. I remembered from the war that most Filipinos spoke English so I knew that later I would be able to make her feel at home. Far be it from me to pressure, to try to make a woman talk if she didn't want to. I had learned that lesson.

Milo stood close to his uncle and Junichi did too. I was

about to open my mouth, to make some kind of welcoming speech, but I was stopped by the sound of voices coming from the way we had come. The reporters had arrived just behind us and came around the corner, their sharp questions a meter or two in front of them. They had been speeding, I was sure, and Junichi had slowed way down, had forgotten his driving, had lost himself in the drama of this new man's story.

*

WHEN a man builds around himself the fragile cocoon of ordinary life, he is inclined to work toward its protection, even if he's been expecting a change. Yet by the time our visitors entered the house the pain and discomfort I had been feeling in my arms and neck had extended into my lower back and legs; it was so pronounced that I could not even pretend to normalcy. I have often been prone to tucking a leg or an arm under me in just the wrong way. Yet it is not the sleeping limb which one dreads, but the awakening, the pain of that limb coming back to life. And the limb in question this time was me, my body, my self. I was awakening and I feared that I might pass away in the process. Death by waking up! Death by the past revisited! My wife's old brother. Who would have thought him alive?

For a day and a half after Ike's miraculous return I tried staying with him, but it was impossible. I couldn't talk to the man, could not bring myself to look upon him as the Ike of my youth, the Ike of thin exuberance and half-made plans. This man was a success, and he was Filipino, not Japanese. The idea of taking up some other national identity as an occupation, a professional practice, was not exactly new to me, but in my own case, at least my hard exterior had maintained itself, at least my basic melancholic self-disdain had survived intact. What was I to do? What was I to say to this foreigner?

I found places in our vast house that I had forgotten, alcoves and cubbyholes that were the outcome of poor design but the vestibules of solitary thought. I could hear the others dancing tentatively at the edges of reunion, but I went to them only when directly called, spoke only when directly spoken to. I was sore of body and spirit, but most of all I was surprised. Throughout my period of self-examination there had been no augury of Ike's return, no thoughts of him floating by with any particular regularity during the past months. True, I had fashioned a solitary life around the semisordid, but I was living my life through, I was law-abiding. Yet now this returner, this foolish parody of MacArthur, this little fat Ulysses, was making my body ache and would make me act. All those years, I began to realize, it was the weight of my failure in the Philippines that I had felt. Yet even now, after everything, I cannot say precisely what my failure was, what my correct action should have been. I had been a victim, like Jimmy Yamamoto, of the situation and of the times. But Jimmy had betrayed me when he died. He had somehow done his duty and I had been left behind, had turned from victim to victimizer with his death. It was all accidental, everything was. Everything that happened to me could have been turned to my advantage by the random altering of events. If Jimmy had not had chocolate to give, if the woman of that small store had not screamed so in the night, if war had not come upon the world, if Los Angeles had contained me, not given me the need to find home elsewhere . . .

But my brother-in-law was in the other room speaking quietly to his sister, my wife. And the probability of an event means nothing after its occurrence. So in my alcove all bundled and hiding I finally decided that the real question, the real concern for me, was this: if Ike, the spirit of a whole generation of Japanese youth, could have changed so completely, then what about Teddy? What about me? Was I such an actor as Ike? What was I, when I left Los Angeles, compared to what I am now? Indeed, my hourglass had run its course. These were profound questions. The first I had had.

The *sensei* came to me often, but when he walked into these dead-end alcoves it was because he had taken a genuinely wrong turn, because he had lost the stairwell or thought he could find some shortcut, some fine passage to new ground. He would sit with me and would gesture, as if about to begin some inescapable line of reasoning, and then the gesture would fall flat and unvoiced into his lap. Once though, just before he was about to return to the living room I decided that I would speak of myself to him. What harm could it do? Though he was a man who spoke constantly, his voice always fell unheeded upon the deaf ears of his adopted family. He could tell my deepest secrets and no one would be able to listen.

"I don't know," I told him. "I could have lived my life so differently. I should have . . ."

"A life comes in stages, Teddy. It is not a whole."

"I, though, have been responsible for the actual deaths of others. In the war . . ."

"Yes," he said. "War is irresponsible. In tea we are never irresponsible as in war."

"I wish he had not come back," I said. "I could have gone on in relative peace, as always."

The *sensei* turned to look at me and said, "Though it was fun going to the airport I've got the feeling he is going to overstay his welcome. It takes too much energy to have to be polite all the time."

The *sensei* was conspiratorial so I said, "I got a double shock at the airport. Not only Ike but that major, the man who brought him off the plane. He was terrible during the war, unreasonable and coercive. I'm sure he sleeps well now, though, his conscience clean."

"It would be something you could ask him," the *sensei* said, "the next time you meet."

I smiled and put my hand on the fabric that covered the *sensei's* arm but he got up quickly then, and went off in the direction he had come.

It amazed me to think that in all the years since the war I could not remember having thought of Major Nakamura even once. Though I had lived with the deaths of Ike and Jimmy I had not thought at all of the possibility that the major could be alive somewhere; worse, that he could be well. Major Nakamura had been such an essential man during those years. He had been all wrong for the job but he had survived it. Perhaps in much the same manner as me.

Suddenly I was visited, there in the alcove of my postwar house, by a strong and a welcome conviction. I was sitting, after the *sensei* left, all slump-shouldered and unhappy, when my mind was swept by a cool breeze that lifted the images of Ike and Jimmy off my agenda and replaced them by a flood of thought about Nakamura. During the war, indeed after it, I had not taken anything to heart, had not done my duty to any country, to any idea, or to any person. But it had not been entirely my fault. At least in part it had been because of him! And what swept through me then was a clear sense of what duty there was left in life for me to do. I would bring my brother-in-law before the cameras to tell the country his story on my show. I would take responsibility for anything that happened, for any turn the show might take, but no matter what the truth about Ike turned out to be, there would also be an unexpected guest of honor. Major Nakamura, not Ike, would be the amateur of that particular hour. In the moments after the *sensei* left, you see, I had been able to focus on what it was I thought my duty should be. For the first time I had been able to name it. And the name that kept resounding in my ears was Revenge.

*

It had been the particular crimes of Major Nakamura that had caused me my years of listless remorse, yet I swear that the truth of it, the fact of his importance in my life, had not occurred to me until the moment I saw him at the airport that day. And even then it had taken some time to distill, some time for me to refine my slow realization. But now I had it firmly in mind. I could have survived the war, not only physically, but with the spirit of my youth intact, had I been subject to the commands of a man with less random brutalization in his policies, with less evil in his dealings with other human beings. And for my pains I wanted nothing more than for him to accept an invitation to be a guest on my show. I would not hurt the man, would give him none of what he had given me. I only wanted to talk to him, to ask him questions, to clear the air.

And so I returned to the living room, where Ike and Kazuko and Milo had been speaking calmly, patiently waiting for me to get my courage up. I found quickly the warmth, the brotherly tones that had been lacking on our ride in from the airport, lacking in the last two days. I sat down and pulled the blanket over my lap, letting the *kotatsu* warm my aching legs. They had been eating *mikan*, so I let my fingers take one from the bowl on the table and practiced a quick removal of its skin. I noticed, because I faced it, that the tokonoma had freshly arranged flowers in it, our best *daruma* scroll hanging behind them. This was my favorite room, the most traditional of the house. Its walls had recently been retextured in the old Kyoto style and the tatami was all fine, strong and new. Still, Ike did not look very Japanese sitting there. His wife and children had re-

tired early. They were not comfortable in these new surroundings and if they saw comfort in the eyes of their
husband and father it made them bitter, reminded them of
the trick he had played.

I smiled, hoping someone else would speak first, and Milo
said, "I was telling uncle that if Junichi were here we could
take an evening drive, see the lights of Roppongi and other
sections."

"That would be fine," I said.

Kazuko realized, in a quick start that reminded me of her
mother, that I had no teacup, that the water in the pot on
the table was tepid. "*Ahra*," she said. She pulled her legs
out from under the *kotatsu* and crawled away before standing. This was like her mother too. "Conversation should
be light and easy," her mother used to say. "It should be
an exercise in helping everyone relax."

Kazuko left quickly and I said, "While it is true, Ike, that
I have not thought of you in years, there are some things
that do not dim to my memory with time. Since you are
here there are things I must tell you."

Milo shifted his weight, uncomfortable with my opening
remark, but though I too wanted everyone to relax, though
I had nothing against my brother-in-law, I did not want to
lose the momentum I had gathered, did not want to become
less single-minded once again.

"Please," said Ike. "I thought you were dead. You thought
I was dead. It is over long ago now. Do you realize how
far that war is from the minds of most people? If we must
talk about war we'd better talk about the next one. Undoing
the past is no solution."

I wanted to argue with him when he said that, for if the
solution to the way we are does not lie in our pasts then
what is the value of trying to change, of trying to remedy
what we have done? But Ike was sitting straighter and had
undone a notch or two of his belt, so I held up my hands.

"What did you find to say to Major Nakamura when you arrived?" I asked. "I had somehow assumed that he was long dead."

Ike was immediately more comfortable. He smiled and said, "I told him '*mabuhay*.' That's a Filipino greeting."

"Nakamura shot Jimmy," I said. "He murdered him."

I spoke slowly and very clearly, and I kept my voice light. But Ike's little foreign-looking smile turned to wax on his lips and he responded stupidly. "I know," he said. "I should not have greeted him so warmly."

Just then Kazuko came back into the room carrying the ingredients for tea on a flat wooden tray. She pushed the tray into the room as a woman in a restaurant might and then slid in after it. When she stood up she stayed away from us for a while, sensing the returned tension. But though Ike's face was serious he waved his hands across the table as if to discount the possibility of any truth in my words. He became strategic. "I want to talk about you for a while, Teddy," he said. "How did you survive? How did you get out of the jungle?" He slumped a little forward, staring through his smile.

Milo was like a man watching a slow and liquid tennis match. He knew his mother wanted him to interrupt but he could not think of a way of doing so. Now Kazuko brought the tea forward tentatively. When she sat back down she began the preparation of the tea without speaking and we all seemed to sense the necessity of waiting as we were until she finished.

"*Dozo*," she said to her brother. "Please," to her son and second husband.

I wrapped my aching hands around the warm teacup and smiled slightly. "It was a handgun, Ike. A small-caliber handgun. The firing point was a centimeter away from Jimmy's head.

"But why?" he asked. "What did Jimmy do?"

"He provided solace to the enemy. He gave candy to an American. He spoke English and was not a strong carrier of the major's convictions."

Ike nodded, almost satisfied, as if the reasons I had given were enough. "He was always like that," he said, and I sneaked a glance at Kazuko before pushing on.

"Therefore," I said, "I had wondered what it was that you and the major found to say to each other. You and he have grown in such different directions. I had hoped to take the occasion of your return to question him a little, to make him sweat."

Had Kazuko been truly like her mother she would have interrupted then, would have introduced some aspect of social grace, making us watchful. But she had just learned, as far as I could remember, for the first time the details of the death of her first husband, the man she had so decisively preferred over me. I picked up my cooling cup and looked at her. "It is Major Nakamura we are discussing," I said. "He has no remorse. Do you remember? We saw him at the airport and he was remorseless."

"Ah," said Ike, "but he could have been acting. He could feel shame under his calm exterior."

"Jimmy would have survived the war if not for him," I said. "He would have been the first to survive."

I was still watching Kazuko but Ike's comment had ignited in me a new strategy and I changed tone. "Yes, Ike," I said. "The major may be as miserable about the war as I have been, if he is acting. And he has had forty years to perfect the role. You might even be able to discern it if you were to see him again."

I waited a moment, hoping that Ike would bring himself farther in. With us at the table were the two other people in the world who had been profoundly connected to Jimmy, profoundly affected by what the major had done. Kazuko's sense of what was happening was evident in the way the muscles at the back of her neck pulled at her downcast head. Why had I not told her before? If she had asked I would have. Perhaps I had relied too strongly, all these years, on my sure knowledge that she would never ask.

Ike laughed and said, "It was unfair of you, Teddy, to have put everything on hold like this until I got back. Since you have, though, we will find out what goes on. Let's pursue it. Let's ask him point-blank."

Ike was tired of the utter seriousness of our conversation and was making an attempt to ease up. Perhaps he thought that by his agreeing with me our little problem would be defused. But at my request Milo hurried into the other room and brought back whiskey and glasses. While Milo was pouring I told Ike about my idea for the television show and secured his agreement to appear. His strategy now was to agree with everything, for if he saw the road ahead as rough he also saw it as short. I knew, of course, even after our brief reacquaintance, that Ike would not have pursued the remnants of war if I had not. His wife and children, asleep in the depths of my house, had no false father, no mere image of a husband in the man. They had the genuine article. It was in his Japanese guise that Ike was most false. Though Ike's English was sharpened by a strict interpretation of vowels, as most Filipino English is, it was his Japanese that let him down. When he spoke Japanese I was embarrassed for him, for he had maintained much of the slang and many of the elements and style that our language took from war. I could even hear, if I listened, the hint of impending victory in his voice. When he spoke of confronting the major he carried a boastful, disquieting quality, which, frankly, I had forgotten.

Nevertheless, we drank well and celebrated our reunion with as much enthusiasm as we could bear. Milo did his best to assist me in maintaining the mood that night. He offered to appear on the show without my having to ask and he led his uncle toward the kinds of conversation that he thought I wanted to pursue. Kazuko stood and brought food and then remained standing, arms folded across her breasts. Ike said he didn't disbelieve what I had said about Nakamura, but how could the man have murdered Jimmy and gotten away with it? The army had been strict and thorough in the discipline of officers as well as men, he assured me, and if Major Nakamura agreed to appear on television Ike would clear the air. He would ask the major what the matter had been, why he had taken the law into his own hands.

And so it was that I learned another of life's little lessons. I did not know, quite, what I had planned for the major were he to appear on my show, but I agreed, in the semilight spirit of the moment, to let Ike approach the major with the invitation. Ike had wanted to go immediately but the cooler mind of Milo convinced him to wait, at least, until morning. The major lived in a town that, though a part of Tokyo, was a long way out, and Ike made me promise that I would awaken him, so that he would be able to get there and back before his wife and children knew even that he had gone. It was a mistake, of course I knew it, but Ike's wartime rhetoric was too tiring to argue down. He felt he had found a way of showing me where he stood. He invited Milo to go with him and poured whiskey, happily, into everyone's glass. Kazuko, by this time, was even farther away from us, on the other side of the room. She was leaning against a wall but was watching her brother, observing the coming action unfold.

*

BUT though we parted in awkward friendliness, though I had made many big decisions, I couldn't sleep, had not, I believe, for days. The muscles of my body ached as if I had recently exercised them and my mind traveled, casting itself upon scene after scene from the near and distant past. I saw Ike's body under the rich jungle topsoil and I heard him using his wartime Japanese to tell me things. "People change," he said. "Don't be so suspicious. It is merely the illusion that they do not that misleads you."

I rose from my *futon* and stood looking out the window of my room at the pale and bluish night. Though it had begun to snow again Kazuko, unconcerned, slept as she always did, her head and neck rising up out of her blankets, balanced upon the little sand-filled pillow that she loved. I bent over, holding my hand above her face, feeling the steady breath of her. Had she changed greatly over the years? She had lost, somewhere, that streak of rebellion that had drawn Jimmy and me to her, that had made her seem different, somehow, from her ancient family.

I did not want to wake my wife so I stepped from the room and slid the door shut behind me. In the hallway I felt a chill from the smooth floorboards beneath my socks, but the winter moon had sneaked in somehow and lit the scene before me, making movement easy. As I progressed along the hall I stood in front of each bedroom door, thinking about the people within, trying to feel the ease with which they slept. In front of Ike's door I felt more anxiety than in other places in the house. The sounds of fitful sleep reached me, the tensions of people at odds. As I stood there I felt sorry for Ike and wondered what greater successes he might have had had he lived his life on familiar ground. His life had mirrored mine, in a way. He too had hidden within the walls of another culture, had married there, had fathered his children, and failed or succeeded all in a country not of his making, not his own. I wonder, would America greet me were I to go back? Did Ike feel welcome here?

In the next room, next to where his uncle slept, was my son. Milo, of course, has a house of his own, but this is his room when he comes home. When our house was newly built and Milo was king, his room was closer to our own, but now it is this larger one that he prefers. I slid the door open slightly and stepped in to watch him sleep, and as I did so Milo pushed his long singer's hair from his eyes. I could see that his mouth was open slightly and that the regular breath that came from it was not bringing him dreams. Milo knows nothing of Jimmy's connection to him. Would Ike's return, I wondered, mean that he would have to know more? It had not been difficult for Kazuko and me to keep Milo's father from him. After all, we ourselves had never discussed it. I think in America such a thing would not be possible but here it did not seem odd. We had not discussed anything but had relied instead on intuition for understanding. And that I am Milo's father is as much a part of Kazuko's mythology as my own.

As I stood there staring I was taken with an impulse to awaken Milo, to talk to him in some deep way, but I did not. Rather I walked quickly from the room and closed the door behind me. Milo said something then, from deep in his sleep, but I could not make out what it was.

In the hallway again I passed quickly by the *sensei's* room and stood at the top of the stairs. Sleep touches the *sensei* so lightly as not to be called sleep at all. At his age, he has said, sleep is only a kind of restful watch, a lookout for whatever messenger death might send. And if he heard me moving by he would want to hover, to plant the awkward seeds of his reasoning in my fruitless mind. So I took care to pass by lightly, and to descend the stairs more with quiet than with speed.

In the room where Ike and I had talked so recently I felt a little better than I had above. This room with its doors to the garden and its tokonoma was my favorite. It was the first built of our house, one that copied the rooms we had lived in before the war. It was the best room, the safest, the kindest of all. In this room I could ask myself questions and know, at least, that the ambience meant me no harm. Though it had been only a few days it seemed far longer since I'd spent my wakeful night alone among Sachiko's trappings. I had known then that something was about to happen, but still I had not been prepared.

I was in the middle of the room, engaged in some unusual clarity of thought, when a slight rattling of the frosted glass on the door drew me. Someone was in our garden. I had no weapon in the house, though what I felt was not very close to fear. There were two figures there. I could see the shadows cast by them and I felt, surely, that they were unaware of me. Burglars were not a problem in Japan; most probably they were drunks, lost on their way home.

I stood closer to the garden door and listened, but they were noiseless. Could it merely be the mindless movements of our fig tree, its flat hands waving in the wind?

The doors to our garden were secured only by a screw, and as I began to turn it I made no effort to be quiet. They would hear me and run into the street, I thought, and I would see them just as they turned the far corner. But though I made noise they wouldn't move. I could have called out, but instead, when the screw was loose, I took the doors in my hands and slid them quickly away from me. There was a bitter cold wind in the garden, the new snow dancing in the air upon it, but the figures paid no attention. Nor were they at all mindful of the noise that I made. They merely stayed where they were, under the fig tree yet slightly over toward the pond.

It was not fear that I felt but a kind of humorous disbelief. The *sensei* and Milo were in the garden, my son upon a high stool, the *sensei* carefully giving him a haircut. Milo's long hair fell onto the snowy ground at the foot of the tree, but though I signaled to them, was about to ask them to tell me how the trick was done, they paid me no attention at

161

all. Milo showed no remorse at the loss of his hair but rather was very serious, very high-minded and resigned. I made a move to step closer but the *sensei* held a hand up to stop me. And it was then that I began to feel a little odd. Milo's hair fell too slowly, each clump of it landing, mortally wounded, upon a bed of dead hair, enough to have come from a hundred such heads.

I did not stand there long, perhaps a minute, but during that time I was transported way back to a time before the war. I felt the breath that I took to be easier, felt the weight of my body less trying on its systems. And I soon saw that perhaps it was not my son and the tea teacher there in the moonlight, but Jimmy and his wife's old grandfather. The house behind me felt calm and assured, the two figures in the garden confident. When the old man finished he found a hand mirror and held it up to Jimmy so that my friend could admire a job well done. And when Jimmy stood and brushed the remaining hair from his clothing they both turned and beckoned toward me. It was my turn, they were saying, come, sit upon the stool in the garden, let them trim my hair away for war.

These were solid figures that I saw, not wisps, not the fog of my imagination. And when I made no move to go nearer they showed some signs of impatience. The younger put his hands on his hips and the elder began tapping his foot on the soft garden ground. Oddly, though, I could hear the tapping just as though it came from the hard metal tip of a dancer's cane. Its rhythm, its marking time, echoed throughout the entire garden, clicked across the fence and down the streets of the neighborhood. Jimmy, who heard the tapping too, took his hands from his hips and began brushing the remaining bits of hair from his clothes. Then he held out his hand, but not to me. He was looking into the darkness near the fig tree where, for the first time, I noticed yet another figure leaning. When he reached out, this figure, that of a young girl, separated itself from the massive trunk of the tree and walked toward him. This figure was all dressed in the darker shades of winter. But she was not Kazuko, not Milo's mother, not Jimmy's wife, and I noticed that the fine bone structure of her face was more like that of the Filipino girl, the one I had met near the jungle years before.

After the girl reached Jimmy I closed the doors on them and quickly turned my eyes back into the common darkness of the room. Apparitions, ghosts, were not to be a part of whatever remedy was in store for me. Mine was to be a controlled return to normalcy, something orderly. As my eyes grew used to the darkness once again I realized that, after all, I had truly not been frightened by what I saw. My house was still my house and the fixtures of this favorite room were still solidly where they belonged. As with Scrooge it could have been something that I ate, a piece of cheese, a bit of underdone potato. I turned in the room, without looking back, and stepped toward the stairs. I was sleepy then and somehow I knew that my little garden party would not venture inside a house where I had sleeping adults whom I could summon, if need be, to calm my imagination or scold these unwelcome visitors and send them on their way.

As I paused before each bedroom door I could hear the sounds I listened for, a throat cleared, a heavy breath, a body turning against the noisy sheets. I was calm again, not startled, and the ache in my muscles had begun to subside. Still, as I walked the remaining distance to my bedroom door I could hear, and stepped precisely to, the impatient rhythm of the old man's cane.

*

I SLEPT without dreams and until the sun was high enough to nudge me back to consciousness with its bright winter

163

light. There's nothing like the vision of dead comrades to destroy the will of the insomniac, to chase him into deep and genuine slumber. But I could not afford, once I had decided upon action, to sit and wonder at the presence of ghosts. I was feeling fine. There was work to be done, a show to organize, the random wills of others to mold to my own. Perhaps these dead friends knew what I was up to, perhaps their presence in the garden was a way of applauding my decision, on a moderate scale, to go to war once again.

I hadn't worried much about Ike's previous evening's posturing until I went downstairs late the next morning to find him gone. I didn't know what effect Ike's visiting Major Nakamura might have on my plan, but when I heard the sound of Milo's car returning I began to feel a little anxious. "Ah," I told myself, "he has probably failed." But when my brother-in-law entered the house I saw, in his heavy eyes, not so much the look of failure as that of defeat. I would have spoken to him but he passed me quickly by, saying only, "I have seen the man and it is true. Though he was a principal once he is a pharmacist now, has been these last few years."

Milo was slower than Ike to reenter the cooling interior of my house. I hadn't thought to tell Milo not to take his uncle to see Major Nakamura, but only because I had assumed he would know better. I was about to speak, about to whisper my surprise at what he had done, when Milo raised his hands, surrendering the point. He poured himself a cup of tea and told me what had happened:

"We stopped at a police box to ask directions," he said. "Nakamura's pharmacy was one of two in the town, easy to find, right off the main road.

"I wasn't clear on what Uncle thought could be accomplished but I couldn't dissuade him, Father, and when we parked the car even Junichi made no move to stay in his seat. It was just six o'clock and I had hoped to use the early hour to temper his insistence. But the lights from the house behind the pharmacy were on and they strengthened his resolve. Uncle took a deep breath and wrapped his knuckles hard against the door. After he knocked again a small light came through the pharmacy, held in someone's hand. 'Wait a minute,' said a woman's voice. 'Who's there?' A small old woman opened the door.

" 'We have come to see Pharmacist Nakamura,' Uncle said, but the woman held up a hand and turned back the way she had come. 'Father,' she shouted. 'Guests. It is early but you've got customers.'

"The three of us stepped inside behind her and Junichi closed the sliding door with care. This was a long and thin pharmacy, Father, full of medicine bottles and pills. And it was poorly kept. Boxes were piled along the walls and everything was dusty."

When Milo stopped for a breath of air and a sip of tea I realized that the story he told had the cadence of something memorized and I could picture him sitting in the back of his car, going over it all during the long ride home.

"There was a man standing back on a tatami platform between the store and the house," said my son. "He was wearing a kimono and had one hand across his brow, making it easier for him to peer at us. When he recognized Uncle he made a slight noise and came down the aisle. He didn't seem surprised or anxious and I even wondered if you, Father, had perhaps called him or something. He shook our hands and then led us back, farther into the store. He had tea water waiting and chairs spread around a gas stove.

" 'Ocha,' he said, smiling at Uncle. 'When the mornings are cold like this it warms me.'

"Uncle started out fairly well by saying, 'It occurred to

me that I didn't have a proper opportunity to greet you when you came to meet me. I wanted this chance to say hello, to ask how you have been.'

" 'I'm a pharmacist now,' said the man. Then he reached back toward a ledge behind him and brought forward a shoebox containing an assortment of sample bottles of tonic and various medicines. 'Be sure to read the labels carefully before you take any of these,' he said, then he handed Uncle the box, letting the bottles sound together within it."

Though my son had never asked a single question about the events that were taking place around him it was clear from the way he told his story that he was going to pretend he knew what was going on. He was going to be my supporter in this, my ally.

"Nakamura smiled," Milo told me, "while Uncle picked up two or three of the small bottles and examined their labels. He had one in his hand when he said, quite casually, 'I did want to ask you about the loss of Private Yamamoto. Do you remember him? He and I were somewhat close and I wanted to ask about his death.' "

"But he was there to extend an invitation!" I said. "Nothing more!" Ike was going to ruin my plan. He was supposed to have gone there only to mention the show!

Milo held up his hand as if asking me to let him finish. "Nakamura remain silent for a moment," he said, "but then he answered Uncle right out. 'The truth about Yamamoto,' he said, 'is that he was insolent. His sympathies should have been questioned long before he was sent to the front like that.' This time when he spoke he struck a posture that was somehow military and I got the feeling he was trying to remind my uncle of the Nakamura he had known. Uncle waited a long time for him to add to what he'd said, but Nakamura would not. He simply smiled across the stove at us, his features presently turning pharmaceutical once again.

166

" 'Did Private Yamamoto do something wrong?' Uncle finally asked. 'I've questioned Teddy Maki but can't get him to tell me much.'

"When Uncle mentioned you Nakamura slapped his hands together loudly, startling us all. He called to his wife for a bottle of sake but there was no response from the back room.

" 'She's deaf,' he told us, 'but she always knows what's happening.' He leaned over and banged the wall once and then smiled hard at Uncle and said, 'That Teddy Maki. I had no idea that my aide, during the war, could turn out to be such a man.'

" 'Teddy Maki and Yamamoto came to Japan together,' Uncle persisted. 'They were members of the same band before the war.'

"Nakamura nodded. 'I used to hear talk of that,' he said.

" 'Then why did you not suspect Teddy too? Why did you punish only the one?'

"Nakamura was really playing with Uncle, I think, but he leaned forward and I got the feeling that he was going to tell the truth. 'I used to be a principal,' he said. 'There were a lot of things that students could get away with in my school, but rudeness wasn't one of them. It was never necessary for the students to respect me personally. I only asked that they respect the office that I held.'

"Uncle leaned forward too, trying his best to keep to the point. 'Yamamoto was rude?' he asked. 'He showed you disrespect?'

" 'Those were long days, you know,' said the pharmacist.

" 'How did he die?' Uncle persisted. 'Did you shoot him?'

"The old man held his chin up again. 'Did my hand hold the gun? Is that what you are asking?' But before Uncle could respond, Nakamura's wife came through the curtain with a bottle of sake and two small cups. 'Ha!' said Nakamura. 'She heard me anyway.' He turned to his wife and frowned. 'You heard me anyway,' he yelled.

"While Nakamura poured the sake a new tension some-how came into the room. I thought that if this Jimmy was murdered there was no doubt at all that it would go un-avenged, but by then I was not sorry we had gone. Nak-amura was pouring sake and smiling at Uncle Ike and the blood was pounding in my ears. I could tell that the sake was cold and I did not want Uncle to drink with the man, but there was nothing I could do to stop him.

"Nakamura sighed and held the little cup out to Uncle and I could feel Junichi's anxiety next to my own. Naka-mura raised his cup, careful not to let the sake ride over the brim. '*Kampai*,' he said. 'Here is to the young man we have been discussing. Though he died long ago he has the advantage of remaining young while those of us he left behind wrinkle around him.' He waited a moment, cup poised, until my uncle raised his own cup straight into the air. Then Nakamura let the sake roll down his throat. Uncle was compelled to do the same, Father, don't you see? He had no choice. The sake was terrible, cold and sweet, I could tell. And when Uncle put his cup down his face was red and I saw small tears in the corners of his eyes.

"Major Nakamura had not misread what Uncle Ike was getting at, Father, I was sure by then. Yet by treating my uncle as a lost comrade he was making it impossible for Uncle to break away. He filled both their cups once more. 'And here is to the original idea,' he said. 'The great East Asia Co-Prosperity Sphere.'

"Uncle drank again, this time, I think, letting the awful taste punish him.

" 'Ah,' said the major. 'Japan is a nation unmatched in the world!'

"As each cupful of sake washed through him the major laughed more heartily, soon even calling for his wife to join them. His pace quickened a little and his voice wove through the room making us all sway. He toasted everything he could think of, the Philippines, the American prisoners of war, the pharmaceutical companies. 'Oh ho,' he said, smiling broadly and pointing his finger through the air until it bumped the front of Uncle's shirt. 'And Teddy Maki! We must not forget him!' He splashed the last of the sake into Uncle's cup. 'He is so funny,' he said. 'Is there no end to the odd things he has on his show?'

"Uncle had not said anything in a long while and had not been drinking much during the last few toasts. He waited until the major held his cup up after toasting you, Father, and then he turned his own cup over, spilling the last bit of sake onto the floor. There was no victory in the move but he did it, perhaps, so that he would be able to call on it later when alone and analyzing the completeness of his defeat.

"Uncle put the cup on top of the stove and when he stood to leave Junichi and I stepped quickly with him, standing as tall as we could. Nakamura didn't move, Father, didn't stand, didn't say anything more. His fist was tight in front of his face, though, and he was staring deeply into it.

"I was the last to leave the building and as I turned to close the door Nakamura's wife ran past me in order to hand the shoebox full of samples to Uncle. They clinked together again, like a parody of wind chimes, and she said, 'That Teddy Maki. I don't like him either but my husband thinks he's great.' "

*

THOUGH he had caused me unexpected problems I could not be angry with Milo after the way he told his story. He had not spoken so much in years! Milo had been moved by his uncle's ordeal, by the surprising defeat of it. And he had observed an event which concerned him far more than he knew. His uncle had traveled with him to extend an invitation which he had forgotten, in his humiliation, even to mention. I understood, after Milo's story, that Nakamura had been ready for Ike and had brought to their confrontation far more skill and energy than Ike had been able to muster. Still it was surprising; a small old man, no longer the leader of warriors, a pharmacist . . .

I left Ike alone with his wounds and told Milo nothing, sending him off with the assurance that I would find a way of getting the stubborn major on the show, some way of getting him before his natural audience. Kazuko was in the room with me after Milo left but I held up my hand so she didn't comment. She was already beginning to adjust, you see, to alter her own frame of mind so that it would suit my own.

Shortly after my son's return I left the house in order to walk and think, and Kazuko, to my surprise, left with me. It had earlier been a habit of ours to take long walks but I could not remember when last we had done so. All during my mistressing, all during the last years of my benumbing middle age, I had forsaken our walks, opting rather for the lazy expanse of the back seat of Milo's car. Yet now, when I took my heavy coat in hand and stepped from the cold antechamber to the street, I found Kazuko by my side. She did not take my arm but I knew she was there. The companion steam of her warm breath stood in the air just at the edge of my peripheral vision.

"I had thought to walk along Meguro-dori," I said. "I need the exercise, the chance to think."

"Meguro-dori has changed," said Kazuko. "It has still not regained itself but it is coming along now. There are many new shops and restaurants."

Before the war Meguro had been a residential area but Meguro-dori, the street itself, had been lively, lined with shops and a joy to stroll down. Kazuko and I walked a long distance without speaking. We passed Otori shrine and then turned when we crossed Yamate-dori, stepping past the site of the Buddhist temple, the one that had burned during the war. There were several new hotels on the property now, small ones renting rooms by the hour or the half-day.

"There used to be a public bath here," I told her, "a rice merchant's there. I remember a very old woman, a friend of your mother. She sold produce, during the war, out of the trunk and back seat of a big old American car."

Kazuko and I walked up along the bank of a drying stream and then down a small bar street with its many-colored doors all closed against the bright winter sun. Though it was still cold and would be for weeks, the day was marvelous, clear and clean. The pace of our walking was sufficient to give us warmth and the sidewalk was bare, empty of debris or ice.

"It is almost Christmas," I told her. "The big department stores in the Ginza will be well-stocked and colorful. We should go down soon, take the train as we used to do, give Milo's car a rest."

For Kazuko Tokyo was really very small. She was a citizen of Meguro, not of the city at large. It may have been months since she had been to Ginza, years since she had ridden the Yama-no-te line, the train that circles inner Tokyo, binding it, defining its size.

"It is good," she let me know, "for old couples to be seen doing such things together. When a man reaches his old age he should have a wife there with him."

Though I had not thought of myself as old before the arrival of my wife's brother, Kazuko said what she did as if we both had known it for a long while and I found myself wondering, suddenly, if she had suffered during my middle age. When her brother and the war and my newly found sense of duty were dead to me, my wife had been too, in a way. Yet I could clearly remember my joy in finding her when I returned so early from the fighting. I remember my surprise at her easy decision to take me in, my pleasure at the stoic and gentle way she wove herself about me. When, exactly, had I begun neglecting her? Had she known about my mistressing? Did she know now that it was over?

As we walked up through some unfamiliar neighborhoods and into the area around Meguro station, I realized that though I was not at peace with myself I was happy. I had much to do and so little time. Perhaps that, not peace of mind, is a proper definition of happiness. I had not had such clear feelings in years. My brain was active, my body alert and no longer sore, the cold winter air a proper tonic. Old age and youth have much in common, are indeed the two tips of the horseshoe in my life, their constructive and destructive natures complementing each other. I had no time to mourn the misuse of my middle age but I did want to take a moment to applaud its passing. My old age, the actions and activities of the next few weeks, at least, would rectify the awful indecision of my youth. And then I would be finished with it, ready to live again. I did not want to lose this clarity of mind, this cool vigor, this welcome change.

We had come to the door of a famous *tonkatsu* restaurant but it was closed. We had been walking for an hour and, though my thoughts had fed me, I was hungry still. Kazuko, I noticed now, had not had an easy time with my pace.

"Here's *Tonki*," I said, "but it's closed. There is no other place to eat around here. Let's take the train."

Kazuko pushed a hand up into the cool air between us. "Wait," she said. "We have not walked this far in years. Let's rest."

There was a stone bench outside the restaurant so we sat down on that. I didn't know what time the place opened. Though I ate there often I had not been up around the station so early in the day in years. We were looking directly through the sliding glass doors, in at the counter where individuals sat to eat.

"We will go for walks like this every day again," I let
Kazuko know. "Now that we are old we need the exercise.
It is the secret to a long and ambulatory life."

Kazuko was so winded that she was not inclined to try
to speak. She had really got out of shape over the years, I
am ashamed to say I hadn't noticed. So while Kazuko sat
still, calming the beating of her surprised heart, I took the
opportunity to try to look at her closely. I stood and walked
over to the restaurant door and then turned quickly back,
imagining that I saw a stranger there. I was trying to make
seeing her fresh, like the view one gets of oneself in an
unexpectedly present mirror. Kazuko had been a beautiful
girl, she had been a coquette with perfect timing in the
pulling of the strings of a young man's heart. Yet as I turned
suddenly upon her sitting there, what I saw was a lady who
could have been her mother's own sister. The years had
drawn upon Kazuko's face similar lines to those her mother
had carried when I remembered her best, during the bombing of Tokyo, during the late years of the war.

I walked a few feet and turned quickly upon her again,
trying for a different view, but Kazuko said, "Stop jumping
about so, Teddy. Sit down and rest," and I could not escape
her mother in the tone she chose.

I smiled and walked over to her. "That stone will make
you cold, Kazuko," I said. "Get up and walk with me."

Kazuko sighed, but she did stand, letting me take her
hand for a few moments while we walked to where we
could catch a bus that would take us back home. Suddenly
I took a step in front of her and turning to face her squarely,
held her shoulders in my hands. "We are old now, Kazuko,"
I said. "You are old and I am too. Your brother has not
returned to us in any real sense, but events are on the
horizon which will set us free. After that we will have each
other for a while."

I don't know what Kazuko had been thinking or how

closely her thoughts paralleled mine, but when I made my little speech she looked at me and started to laugh. And even when the bus came she was not inclined to cover her mouth or lower the steady and mirthful gaze of her eyes.

*

In honor of my awakening, in honor of the decisions I had made, I bought a large and wonderful Christmas goose. It had been hanging in the doorway of a butcher shop and I had walked past it several times admiring its full size, the solid good color of its skin. I had been thinking that it might be difficult now to get Major Nakamura down to my studio and I'd convinced the producer, without telling him too much, that such a show as we had planned would be better accomplished if we were to go on location. "We'll catch him in a position of relaxed prosperity," I said. "He is no longer a soldier but a pharmacist. He will contrast well with the odd changes that have occurred in my brother-in-law." The goose was to be the bait. The good Christmas tidings, delivered by me like Scrooge.

I had always had a free hand at the studio, but organizing what we called a "remote" took time and careful planning. I wanted to cast the show, to choreograph it, so as to make it both dramatic and entertaining. This was not to be mere revenge but good television as well, a clear departure from my usual fare. I took some time to think about it, then one day I asked Junichi to rummage around in the costume room, to find authentic old army uniforms for us all to wear. My audience, I hoped, would be intrigued by my change of format. The show would be different, better than anything I had ever done. Even the *sensei*, though I wasn't sure why, would appear on camera. With Nakamura, there would be six of us in the production. I had decided not to contact the major or to give him any advanced notice. We would merely arrive, one day, with our cameras. I was relying heavily on the goose to get us through the door. Food is rarely a sign that an enemy has arrived.

The day I chose for our visit to Nakamura's drugstore was Christmas Day itself, not a particularly important day in Japan, but ironic to what was still American in me. Kazuko and Ike's wife fixed us a large breakfast and there was much laughter, much nervous chatter, such as I had remembered soldiers sometimes had before entering battle. The studio van was in front of my house early, the cameramen and electricians already somewhere near the drugstore in one of the studio trucks. I didn't know what I was going to do if the show was a failure or if Nakamura refused to let us in or if, in fact, he wasn't home. This last possibility bothered me greatly so I took a moment, before we left the house, and dialed his number from the telephone in the back bedroom. It was quite early in the morning but the phone rang only once before Nakamura plucked it from its cradle and spoke.

"Yes, this is Nakamura," he said.

I waited, not responding, until he spoke again. *"Moshi moshi? Nakamura desu."*

"Ah," I said. "I am calling someone named Nakamura but I fear I have made a mistake."

"There are many Nakamuras," said Nakamura. "Which one are you calling? What number did you dial?"

His voice was helpful and friendly. He was a man whose day was starting well, a man who had time enough to talk at length with a stranger.

"I am calling Nakamura the pharmacist," I said. "Nakamura the school principal."

"Yes," he said. "You've got the right man. This is Nakamura."

"In that case," I told him. "I am coming to make a delivery. I trust you will be at home?"

There was a moment's silence then, when I began to feel that I had been foolish to call.

"Who is this?" the pharmacist asked. "I ordered nothing, am expecting no delivery. Who is speaking?"

"The Nakamura I want was a major, a man of heavy responsibilities during the war," I said.

"Identify yourself," he said. "I am Major Nakamura but who are you? Who is calling me?"

Now it was my turn to pause. I regretted the call but I had needed to know that the man would be home. His voice had thus far remained even and calm.

"Major Nakamura," I said. "This is Maki and I am coming to give you the gift of a Christmas goose, the finest I could find."

There was silence again so I very quickly and lightly let the phone slip back onto its cradle. I had planned the day carefully and knew then that the major would be waiting. I had given him a warning, something that I realized I had wanted to do all along. There had been no fear in the major's voice, no apprehension. When I came out of the bedroom Kazuko was there and told me that the others had already gone outside, were waiting in Milo's car. She had wrapped the goose for me in bright red and green gift paper and had placed it in a large basket that rested at my feet.

*

Milo's car held us lightly, better than it had when, so recently, we all drove back to town from the airport. It was not my idea that Ike's entire family, people I had yet to really speak to, should be going, but neither did I feel a need to force them to stay at home. Kazuko, I think, had arranged it all. Though Kazuko spoke no English, in the short time since her brother's arrival, she had managed to befriend her brother's wife, to teach his children the words of endearment she wanted them to use when calling her. This time Junichi and my son and I sat in the front seat of the car. But though there were seven of them in the back they seemed spread out, casual in the postures they chose. There was not the confinement of a first meeting.

When we got to the major's town, one of those small subsections of Tokyo in which many people live, Junichi found the studio van and truck and pulled directly in behind them. The drugstore, Milo told me, was close by, out of sight but just around a corner.

"The men have business in the van for a while," I said. "Women and children can wait on the sidewalk, but please, not near the entrance to the store."

Although it was early, townspeople were on the streets. There were no shops opened but there were walkers, and Kazuko and Ike's family had no trouble joining in. They turned away and began a leisurely stroll down toward a Shinto shrine on the corner. They weren't nervous about the show. I was sure they didn't realize what it all might mean.

Once inside the van the men chuckled at each other much as men have always done when women leave them in charge of the hunt. Electronic equipment filled nearly half the van and Junichi's clothing rack, one he'd lined with old studio uniforms, took up much of the rest of the space. Now we were crowded, stood too close to each other, found, with the departure of one half our group, that we could not turn about freely, could not talk in the unrestrained manner that I had been anticipating. Through the van's front window I could see that the cameramen were dressed and ready to go. They looked odd in the uniforms they wore. I hadn't realized that Junichi would designate the cameramen as soldiers too but I understood that my son's chauffeur, like Milo himself, was of an unthreatened age, one for which war was not a possibility. Perhaps this exercise, then, was his chance to imagine what it had all been like, to remember, in a way, the glory of it.

"Each has his own uniform," Junichi said. "Never mind the rank, they were chosen according to size."

Junichi was slow and gentle in the way he took the uniforms down and passed them to us, and I could see a certain light shining in his eyes. These uniforms had been washed and pressed by him, yet they were the uniforms of television soldiers, not of real ones. Where buttons and belts should have been, on these uniforms there were only Velcro strips. One folded one's uniform around oneself and then firmly pressed it into place. It was more like being wrapped up than like putting something on, and I remembered the Christmas goose which we had left in the trunk of Milo's car.

Though there was little space we dressed quickly, letting our morning clothes fall to the floor of the van in a heap. Junichi had said that rank was not of any consequence in this army, but I could not help noticing that both Ike and I, the primary actors, were privates (indeed, that is all we had ever been), while Junichi and Milo were military police. My son's uniform even had a microphone placed in a Velcro band around his waist. The shoulder pads of his uniform were extra large, making him look athletic, and each contained a loudspeaker. Presumably this policeman could be called out during situations where magnification of voice was paramount; when asking television criminals to come out of buildings or when negotiating with the enemy across an expanse of open and hostile land. The *sensei*, alone among us, wore the insignia of an officer. Junichi helped him put them on correctly and the old man smiled. "I won't disappoint you," he said.

We were dressed, caps in hands, and about to step from the van, when I decided that I should say something about how we would proceed. I didn't want to inhibit my friends but we were not all professionals. I had never seen Ike act (had I?) and I was worried about what things, unexpected, the *sensei* might say.

"We will enter the store with our cameras running," I told them. "Let us take our lead from what the pharmacist says. If he is hostile we will respond kindly; if he is kind we will raise our questions bluntly."

No one appeared to be about to comment so I shrugged and passed around a small hand-mirror so that they might all look at themselves. When Ike put his cap on his head I felt like greeting him. This was the man I had expected at the airport, the soldier hidden for so long. The door to the van was opened, but before we stepped to the street, my son twisted the many strands of his long hair under the cap he wore. The effect was phenomenal, but the change did not seem to draw the attention of any of the others. Milo had become my garden visitor of a few nights before. I looked carefully at my son and, though he was unaware of his new role, his young face brought my heart to my throat, my pulse to the very threshold of my eyes. Something was afoot in the outside world, the one not under my control. With his jaw set the way it was, Milo was Jimmy's double and I began to worry a little about what was in store.

Those of us in uniform looked odd on the street but we practiced control, pushing ourselves into the roles of soldiers. The women and children were back and waiting, and when the cameramen saw us they stepped down from the back of the truck, holding their cameras at odd angles, like machine guns. We had decided ahead of time that Ike's children would wait for us outside, either on the street or in the back of the van where they could see and hear everything that would go on. As for Ike's wife, she could do as she pleased. Kazuko had given her a kimono to wear and she looked fine, younger and more reasonable than had been my earlier impression of her.

Ike said something to his children and they quickly went through the van door and closed it behind them. They were well-behaved children and for them, I thought, this new world must be something unfathomable. They had been the children of an ordinary man only a few weeks before. And now they could, no doubt, see us moving across the television monitor. Would their father seem foreign to them as he marched so resolutely away?

"All right," I said. "Follow the lead of good show business but do not let the man coax you from the point of our visit."

One of the cameramen moved around the corner in order to take our picture as we approached. Already a small crowd had formed. Onlookers. An audience. The front of Nakamura's drugstore was in worse condition than I had imagined from Milo's earlier description of it. It was narrow and dark, the sign bearing his name hanging loose and in need of repair. When we arrived at the front door I knocked immediately and then called out. The store, of course, might be closed all day, but I could see lights through the frosted glass. I was about to call again when the door slid away from my hand. An old woman was standing before me. She was dressed very finely, as if about to go out, as if the day were New Year's Day, not Christmas at all.

"He is not here," she said. "He told me to greet you and to tell you that he is in the warehouse at the back. If you like I can take you there."

The old woman spoke passively, so as not to jar the perfect arrangement of her hair. She did not shy from the camera's red eye, nor did she say anything about the clothes we wore. She merely moved to let us know that we were to follow her through the drugstore and toward the back.

Along the aisle of the store were the advertisements Milo had mentioned, but to my eyes they were cracked and faded, many of them out of place or falling down behind the shelves. Nakamura's store was very poorly kept. There was dust on all the bottles, and along the counter top at the back I could see heavy streaks in the uneven light. I could see the imprints of Nakamura's hands where he'd placed them while leaning there over the years. This was a store that had not changed since before the war; it had an old-fashioned layout, a dark and medicinal feel.

We followed the old woman past the counter and through the curtains that separated the store from the living quarters at the back. We walked past the tatami room where the Nakamuras slept, stepping lightly over the small squalor that spilled out into the hallway. We passed a dingy kitchen where they made their food and heated water for tea. Brown, crusted rice lay on the small kitchen table. Bits of it had fallen to the floor and stuck to the soles of our shoes as we passed by. Somehow I had supposed that Nakamura had been successful, that he was affluent. After all, forty years had passed and he had been a school principal before that. I'd thought of him as successful during a time when Ike and Jimmy and I had still been boys.

As we approached the end of the building, the old lady turned and spoke. "He stays in the warehouse on holidays," she said. "He doesn't like the inactivity of a day to ourselves."

Out the back door of the building was a surprisingly large garden which was, in contrast to the rooms we'd just passed through, neat and well manicured. The path we stood upon was made up of hundreds of small round stones and the garden itself contained many shades of fine and cultivated moss. We wanted to fan out, once we had the space, but we stayed on the path. We were soldiers who respected the traditional landscaping of Japan and Nakamura, if in fact he had done the work himself, was truly an expert. His trees were trimmed perfectly and he had devoted a small portion of the garden to a few fine large boulders in a sea of raked gravel. Here was the energy that I had expected would go into his store.

"Father is expecting you," said the woman. "There. In our warehouse."

She pointed as she spoke, out the back gate, at a huge building which stood in a field across the narrow alley. What would a pharmacy of such derelict quality need with a warehouse so large? We bowed to the woman and thanked her, but one of the cameramen had knelt by the side of the garden and was focusing his lens deeply into a bed of moss, so we had to wait. Though it was still early in the morning the winter chill had left the air and the sun had risen over the fence that surrounded us. Kazuko and Ike's wife had moved toward the front of our group, letting the soldiers fall in behind them. Kazuko looked at the woman. "A garden such as yours is so rare these days," she said. "Who took the time to work at it so finely?"

The woman blushed when Kazuko spoke but said, "My husband and I work at it together. Often we kneel beside each other looking for weeds, for the undesirables that might ruin a garden like our own."

The soldiers kept nonspecific looks on their faces while the women spoke, but the second cameraman let his camera run, taking in everything the women said or did. The warehouse loomed above us, making me feel small. Finally Nakamura's wife said, "Please, he will be growing impatient." She pulled the thin rope that opened the latch on the back gate and we all stepped through into the alley. The warehouse had previously been used for the storage of sake. There were various markings on the walls and there was an old, crippled wagon in the tall grass beside the door. Nakamura's acumen for gardening did not extend, I could see, so far as the edges of his warehouse. The building itself was made of stone and had a new wooden roof where, certainly, straw had once kept things dry.

"It is a family warehouse," said Nakamura's wife. "His grandfather used it long before the war. Of course we don't need so much space to store our meager drugs. Father uses it as his retreat now. He has it fixed up just the way he likes it and comes here often to relax and meditate."

Ike and Milo and the others had been suspended in silence all during our walk through the building and out the back and I remembered regular military patrols. Though we expected action at any time it always came as a surprise. The major's wife pulled a heavy chain on the front of the door, allowing it to swing out until it blocked, partially, the alley between the warehouse and the gate leading to their home. She stood back and bowed in a formal way and spoke once more. "Go now," she said. "Step inside."

I had only called the man to insure that he would be home, to insure that he would be present for our questions if not agreeable to answering them. Yet it appeared as though I had given him time to set something up. Was this to be an ambush? Had he his own private army ready to attack us from the rafters?

We passed through the entrance then quickly moved into a crescent, fanning out and crouching. Nakamura's wife closed the big door. "Father," she said. "You were right. Guests have arrived."

The entire warehouse, ceiling, walls, and floor, had been painted stark white and there were dozens of high-wattage light bulbs hanging down on six-foot cords from the thirty-foot-high ceiling. The place was built like a theater. There were crates standing freely here and there, and there was a high platform at the back of the building, a stage on which several chairs had been placed.

I spoke. "My friends and I are not enemies," I said. "We

have come with microphones to document what we say, cameras to show that we mean no harm."

My voice carried so well within the warehouse. I had not shouted yet could be heard in the farthest corner of the building, I was sure. "We are not military men but wear these clothes only to remind you of the time of which we wish to speak."

Nakamura was not visible but it did not occur to me to doubt that he was there. I could feel his presence, was quite certain he was standing behind one of the crates waiting to make his entrance. His sense of timing was turning out to be well tuned. We were the entertainers, not this pharmacist, yet he controlled us with his silence.

"Surely," I said, "you will not deny us an interview. We have not spoken since the war, you and I. There is much we might find to say to one another."

"No doubt," said a voice, its words low and carefully spoken.

"I cannot tell where you are standing," I said. "Show yourself."

The cameramen held their cameras low and Ike motioned to the others in ways he had perfected during his short weeks as Nakamura's aide. "Spread out," he seemed to be saying. "Stay down. Keep your eyes open."

Nakamura spoke. "My ancestors have always lived here, in and around this building. They were involved with grain once, and then with spirits. Now you and I are involved with spirits of a different sort. Why don't we let them rest? We are too old to be engaging in such difficulties."

The light in the warehouse, now that the door had been closed for a while and my eyes had adjusted, was strangely even. Though there were circles of it, the products of the hanging bulbs, there were so many of them that there was a blend. Nakamura's wife was standing behind me and spoke to Kazuko.

"Father has not been well," she said. "Had he his health, he would have remained a principal."

The woman's voice bothered me so I raised my own. "Major Nakamura, it is Christmas Day," I said. "Are you dressed as well as your wife?"

"More finely, even, than that," he said.

Nakamura's voice, though we had no trouble hearing it, was so low that I got the impression he was involved in some activity, speaking to us with his back turned. I was growing impatient with him and motioned to the others. We all walked forward in an ungainly way. Soldiers, when before a finer presence, have always tended to be clumsy. Still, we walked nearly to the front of the building hoping to force the issue. I began to notice that there were *zabuton* on the floor all around us.

Suddenly Nakamura stood on the stage, perfectly in view from our new vantage point. He had not moved, I understood, but had been there all along. He had merely come into view in this odd room. Some trick of the lighting had hidden the spot where he stood. When I saw him I felt a chill. Truly Major Nakamura wore a fine holiday kimono but upon his face, covering entirely the look I had anticipated seeing, was a fine, white, even and expressionless Noh mask. He was dead still and staring at us.

"This is not a play," I said.

"I was cast upon foreign soil as the leader of men," said Major Nakamura. "This is no less a play than that was."

Nakamura moved his body slightly when he spoke, as Noh actors do. He tipped his head so that the light played upon the mask, giving expression to it. There was something to be seen there; the sense of a frown, a smile in moderation.

"The *zabuton* are for the audience," he said. "Actors should be on the stage."

"Come," I said, but the others were already by my side,

the women already sitting upon the large and comfortable looking *zabuton*. The stage was chest-high, not an easy climb, but before I could say anything Junichi and Milo had hoisted themselves upon it and were giving the rest of us a hand. They lifted the *sensei* off the floor with delicacy. They reached down for Ike with strong, assured hands. I was the last to be pulled up to the high platform upon which the action would take place and I felt flushed and disoriented. Our host, in his mask, had remained perfectly still. There were five chairs and, without instruction, we all sat down.

Once my senses cleared I noticed that next to Nakamura yet slightly toward the back of the stage was a long table covered with Noh masks. I couldn't see them well but I could tell that they were of many shades and that their frozen expressions were varied. In a moment Nakamura turned and stepped slowly forward, lifting his arms, in their kimono sleeves, high out from his sides as he did so. Why had I assumed that his life, these forty years, had been a normal one? Clearly he had lived a horrible life all these years. This was his collection, his hobby. What Nakamura had created could only have been the labor of years, could not have been prepared solely for his meeting with us this Christmas Day. Perhaps he had lived all his life, since the war, under Noh masks, in this warehouse of his.

"Major Nakamura . . ."

"You are all soldiers come to remind me of the war," he said. He kept still when he spoke, kept his arms raised like that, his kimono sleeves drooping like wings.

"My son and brother-in-law visited you once before," I said softly. "We come now out of curiosity, out of a need to bury old memories."

"Do not lie," said Nakamura.

"Here is my son," I said. "Here is my brother-in-law. I am not lying."

I stood up and turned to my left and right and Milo and

Ike stood too. We took a step toward the major. We moved in unison, felt the solid construction of his stage floor beneath our feet.

Major Nakamura dropped his arms abruptly then and spoke, from behind his mask, in a normal voice, one I actually recognized from the past. "What is it that you want?" he asked. "I can do nothing for you."

"We cannot forget what happened to Private Yamamoto," I said. "I remember the day you shot him. It has stayed with me all of my life ruining my ability to be free."

"You lay too much blame on Yamamoto," he said.

Though the major's voice remained normal, the empty stare of his Noh mask was inhibiting my line of questioning. I stepped closer to him and held out my hand.

"I was there, major," I said. "I remember the way you raised your arm, the way your pistol came to the side of his head. I remember the way he fell to the ground and died."

"You are a fool, then," he said, "to have wasted your life holding that thought. You were a mere observer, a member of the audience like these women here. Would it be their fault if I shot you now?"

Junichi, perhaps hearing the major's words as a threat, stood and took a careful step forward, but I persisted. "Have you thought about Private Yamamoto over the years?" I asked. "Or is he buried among the relics of your past?"

The major raised his arms again and tipped his mask up toward the light before answering my question. He recited a famous poem.

> "*Tired of cherry,*
> *Tired of this whole world,*
> *I sit facing muddy sake*
> *And black rice.*"

The poem, rendered in the strangest and most wayward of voices, moved the last of us, the ancient *sensei*, out of his chair.

"I remember that poem," he said. "It is true. So true."

Though Nakamura's presence before us was frightening, the *sensei* stepped up to him with no hesitation. "I have seen many Noh plays," he said, "but I have never acted. How is it that you stand? What is it that you do with your hands?" The old teacher walked back to the long table, but waited until he was sure Nakamura would raise no objection before picking up one of the masks. He did not fasten it to his head, as the major had done, but merely held it to his face, peering through it with his ancient eyes. "There is one play I know," he said. "Recite a little with me." He held a thin hand out then and began to hum, modulating his voice as the major had. "*Oooo,*" he said. "*I was by your side in youth. Do you not remember me? I have remained in spirit form, dwelling in the furthest reaches of your garden. . . .*"

Though I was irritated at my loss of control I was stopped by the voice the *sensei* had mustered. Could everyone act, then? His words were barely discernible under the mews and brays of his style.

The major remained motionless for a long moment but finally answered the old man, slumping under the weight of his words as he did so.

"*I remember you,*" he said. "*You are the spirit of young Lord Bando, keeper of my master's hopes, carrier of his name into antiquity. Why do you not rest? Why do you remain in the garden?*"

The women, familiar with the lines, crooned their approval from down below the stage and the *sensei* said, "*I have watched my father's house decaying from my place in the garden. . . . Yet it is not unrestful.*"

The major swung his arms then, so that his kimono sleeves ballooned out in front of him. He took a step toward the edge of the stage and peered out across the warehouse. "*I *can hear your voice,"* he said, *"but I can see nothing of you. When I am restless and the moon is high I have seen you, though, staring up toward the house."*

"If you can see me I am real," said the *sensei.* *"If you can hear me I am real of voice. If you can neither see nor hear me then I have gone to my grave, as you wish, to rest."*

The warehouse amplified perfectly the lines from the play. I could not have remembered the lines myself but knew, when I heard them, that they had been spoken correctly. Had Major Nakamura practiced Noh as therapy, then, much as I had haunted the edges of Sachiko's wounds?

I stepped between the actors. "Enough," I said. "We have not come to hear Lord Bando but to remember the equally youthful death of Private Yamamoto. His ghost does not wait in the garden at my house. His voice does not echo across the years." My own voice did, though, across the warehouse when I spoke.

All of a sudden Ike came forward, grim-faced with determination. "We want to know exactly why you shot our friend," he demanded. "No more talk. You must tell the nation the reasons for your behavior!"

It was clear, when he spoke, that Ike was no longer Japanese. Either that or we were not. He had forgotten the rhythms of things and spoke so much like a World War II soldier that I feared he might actually strike the major. Junichi moved closer to him. No one in Japan spoke like that anymore. Noh plays still moved us but the rhetoric of war did not.

There was a quiet moment then until my son stepped forward and said, "Here. Let's pretend. Let me take the part and see what I can do with it." Milo took the Noh mask from the *sensei* but waited, not raising it to his face. With his hair under his hat he too was a fearful sight and I could tell that Major Nakamura was afraid of Milo, thought we had brought him Jimmy's ghost to serve our purposes.

"I am the same young man who visited you with my uncle," Milo said. "We are all modern people wearing stage uniforms. Noh is not popular in Japan anymore. You could remove your mask without risk."

"It is my only hobby," said the major. "How could I remove it?"

"We will be gone shortly if you tell us about the day in question," said my son. "That day when you killed my father's friend . . . I am not taking sides, you understand. Tell us the story from your own point of view."

Milo looked so much like Jimmy, stood so calmly, spoke so nicely to the major, that I began to feel the beginning of an unraveling.

Major Nakamura spoke slowly. "There was a prisoner," he said.

"Yes," said Milo. "An American."

"He was not humbled by his defeat, would not act as if defeated."

"An American still," said Milo. "That is what they do."

Junichi, tallest among us, lifted the most foreign-looking of the masks from the table. He held it up and looked defiantly through it, trying to help things along.

"Yes," said the major. "Like that."

"But he was your prisoner," said my son. "His defiant look would not give him any more freedom. He had no weapon, other than that look. You had his freedom under your control."

"It was the situation," said the major. "He was defiant before a backdrop of thin and beaten men. He was thin and beaten also but that look denied it. It was a look he had stolen from his captors and I thought it might give the other prisoners something to hope for."

"He wasn't facing reality, is that it?" asked Milo.

"Life was tedious then," answered the major. "I was its administrator."

Milo turned a moment, to stare out over the warehouse, then he looked back at the major and the rest of us. "OK," he said. "Let's run through it once. Show us where we should stand. Your point of view is coming clear to me but I need things spelled out."

"It is too painful," said the major. "The stage is barren, leaving too much to the imagination."

But Milo took Junichi by the arms and stood him alone at the center of an imaginary circle in the center of the stage. The mask Junichi had chosen was that with the whitest of skin, yet one with the hint of a smile. It was a clown's face with one eye circled thinly in black. Junichi let his arms hang loosely at his sides and hunched his shoulders up around his neck so that the mask looked perched upon them.

"You see," said Milo. "He does not elicit sympathy. He looks wild and foreign." Milo affixed the mask to Junichi's face and pressed his chauffeur's arms to his sides once more for emphasis. Then he took the toe of his boot and, dragging it as a cripple might, reinforced the imaginary circle in our minds.

"Very well," said the major. "I am standing him in the yard to break his spirit. It worries me that he has lasted so long. You have been given the job of guarding him. You are feeding him candy so that his spirit will be bolstered. What makes you think that you can do that?"

Instead of answering the major, Milo turned to look directly at me. And then slowly he raised the Noh mask, fastening it to his face. I could not see my son in that final look he gave me. I could only see Jimmy. Yet when the mask covered my son's face the power of the moment increased. His was the most classical of masks, the one most devoid of carved emotion. Now all three of them wore masks. They were all of a piece, gone from the rest of us. The major seemed to calm under the inevitability of it all.

"It was a hot night and I was pulled to the window of

my office often," he said. "I could see you carelessly standing with your rifle in your hands. The prisoner's face was
reflected in the moonlight, but yours, as always, was in the
shadows."

"I was merely doing my job," said Milo. "I gave him
nothing to hope for."

"What you gave him was sweet and I wanted him to learn
a bitter lesson," said the major. "You gave him hope itself."

"Death was everywhere," said Milo, "but perhaps when
I gave him candy he did not think he was going to die. It
was not hope but only a thought. Was that too much?"

The two of them had been speaking normally, standing
firmly upon the stage, but I began to see the dusty landscape
of the Philippines before me once more. The even lights of
the major's warehouse became the hot spotlight of the major's prison. The American prisoner hung before us by some
thread of reserved strength but was so weak he was ready
to fall forward into the dust. Clearly the candy had done
him no real good, yet his face still held a distant and be-
guiling look. If it was not defiance it was something close,
disrespect, perhaps, or superiority. The major let the lilt
of Noh bother his intonation once again. He seemed to
realize that he had been cast as evil and put, at least, his
voice into it.

"I will not have the outcome changed," he warned. "You
should go back now whence you came, before it is too late."

"I am here to represent my father," said Milo, and as he
spoke, though I had not seen him move, his face turned
darker.

"The uniform you are wearing makes me remember that
you were a common private," said the major. "Do you think
that by changing clothes you can judge me? You have no
authority here."

The two men had remained so still that what Milo did
then, though slight, was startling. He took a quick step in

the direction of the major, away from the American prisoner in the circle. And when he stopped he removed the small microphone from the belt of his uniform and spoke into it. "Nothing you can do will alter the events, major," said my son. "It is that you *cannot* change the outcome, not that you will not have it changed."

The major, in his own turn, was swift then, for while we were all caught up in the echo of Milo's words, in the loud magnification which came from the speakers in his shoulder pads, Major Nakamura reached inside the breast of his kimono and knocked the microphone from Milo's hands with a suddenly appearing gun.

"Very well," he said, turning the butt of the pistol immediately in the direction of my son. "Here is your weapon. Shoot him. Shoot him now." The microphone had fallen to the floor and slipped away from the action in a slither of sound. It was a noise that made my spine tighten.

Milo was languid in taking the pistol from the major's hand, but once he had it he walked directly over to the American officer and placed the cold barrel against his head, just above his ear.

"What would you have me do?" he asked.

"Shoot him," said the major.

Milo pulled the hammer of the pistol back but then stayed his finger, letting it rest near the trigger but not letting it touch. "I will carry out your order," he said. "But is there to be no blindfold?"

The major was stopped by what my son said but caught his breath for only a second.

"Maki," he said, "bring a blindfold. Bring something with which to pin it behind this man's head."

When I heard my name I froze, though it had become terribly hot under the lights. They were only acting but what was I to do? Was I to enter in? I had no mask.

"Maki!" shouted the major. "Do as I say!"

I stepped forward. "There is nothing, major. There are no blindfolds."

"Yes there are!" the major shouted. "There were blind-folds!"

"I await your orders," said my son. "What is it that you would have me do?"

Major Nakamura wheeled around, staring once toward the audience, once toward the lights that burned from above. "Shoot him, then," he said. "Shoot him now!" But Milo had released the tension in his arm and let the pistol come, still in his hand, down to his side.

"You see," shouted the major. "It was insubordination! I was within my rights! Then as now it was war. I was the commander of all these men!"

The major took the pistol from Milo's hand quickly then, and pointed it at my son's head. And before I could do anything he pulled the trigger, sending a vast and horrible amount of sound spinning toward the ceiling of the room. It had happened again! I opened my mouth and felt the launching of my son's name from the very floor of my soul. "MILO!" I screamed.

"*Milo!*" the warehouse answered back.

I fell to my knees just as Milo fell, in his slow descent, to land, arms akimbo, upon my lap. But the bullet, this time, had not been aimed as perfectly as before. The major, wherever he had aimed, had sent a glancing shot off the wooden forehead of the perfect mask that Milo wore. The mask split evenly down across its nose and through the red and tightly pursed lips. And as I sat there staring I saw my son's real face again, born from under his murdered one. There was a mark on his forehead, a bruise, but the bullet had gone somewhere else, flying off into space with its sound.

There was commotion and I was aware that the pistol had been taken out of the major's hands. Milo's face had been sweating terribly so I pulled the Velcro stripping and let the jacket fall away from his chest. He was breathing normally, slowly getting ready to open his eyes, when I looked up and saw that Junichi, so brave and loyal, was still wearing the mask of the American soldier, the white man's mask with its little bit of defiance across the nose and mouth. This time he had survived the war and had in his hands the microphone, the one the major had knocked away from Milo. He held the microphone to his mocking mouth and tipped his head toward the light as he spoke. "All soldiers die," he said. "None of them are guilty." His voice, of course, came from my son, who was alive and sleeping across my lap, his long hair dangling down from beneath his cap.

*

THE Kado is closed now, its clientele gone down the road, but we are all inside awaiting this evening's broadcast of my show. Everyone is at a loss as to what to say. The keys to the bar are on the counter next to a note from Sachiko explaining that she has gone back to Hiroshima for a while. She has taken the cash receipts and left the rest to me, so that, at least, has made things easier. I will probably sell the bar, though it has not been a bad business and its location is just right.

Kazuko has cooked the goose we forgot to give the major and it is standing on the counter now, next to Sachiko's note. Were there customers the goose would go quickly but since we are alone in the bar I cannot predict that it will. We are not hungry. Nor are we drinking heavily in anticipation of how the nation will take such a display as they are about to receive.

It has been nearly a week since we went to the major's warehouse for our strange encounter with the past, and during that time Milo and I have kept ourselves busy with the editing of the show. Milo, in fact, has been all business. He has changed. His critical eye is so vastly improved that I think it must be Jimmy's final legacy to him. In case after case, during the week, Milo made choices without waiting first to see where I stood on the matters. And he viewed the final wounding scene, the one where the major would have murdered again, with so much cool distance, so much objective balance, that I thought for a while he had forgotten his part in it. Only once, during our editing, did I speak to my son of the war, and then I admitted to him that Major Nakamura was not the only murderer onstage that day. I told Milo the story of what happened after Jimmy was killed, of how I was singularly unhesitant in putting a bullet through the head of the man Junichi had so mournfully played, the American captain from Los Angeles. My weapon had been a rifle, I told my son, longer and more finely aimed than the major's poor handgun. I let him know that the American was weak and blinded and I told him that I had known what the American was thinking at the precise instant of his death: He was picturing his family and my bullet divided the scene for him, cutting through his thoughts like scissors through a family photograph.

I had been wondering, this week, whether Major Nak-amura's condition has always been worse than my own or whether we moved him to it with our warlike arrival at his store. His wife had said that he was not well, but by comparison to what we found my own eccentricities are mere duck spittle. We left him alone, you know, when we carried Milo from the building, no one saying anything more. So far as I know he may still be wearing his mask, may still be sitting, all hunched up, his mind in the Philippines, his body on the floor of that warehouse of his. Should I feel better after having riled a mad old man? There was never anything in all of this so simple as revenge. What I got, in the end, was a verdict on my own behavior, that is all, a final *Not Guilty* after all these years. And I am only hopeful, now, that I might live to be the *sensei*'s age, that the events of a week ago will have time to mend me well before I die.

It is oppressive in this bar; the others feel it as much as I. Ike is sitting in the corner separated by a short distance from his ever-silent wife and children. He has told me, though Kazuko doesn't know it yet, that he and his family will be returning to the Philippines when all the public interest in him has died away. He should not have come back, he said, and I told him that I knew he was right. It was only his illness that brought out whatever in him has remained Japanese, and he should continue his healthy life now that he is well again. Isn't it amazing? A man returns to his native land after many years nurturing a disguise. But when he is finally home, finally among his family once again, the disguise will not be removed. Where is the disguise? Where is the real man? As Ike sits so undemonstrative at the bar I have to wonder when he will begin to ask those questions of himself. When he gets home where will home be, how far will it have gone from him?

Junichi has been eating more of the goose than any of the rest of us. He has made several sandwiches and taken them behind the bar with him where he is setting the dials on the television set and turning the volume high. None of us, it appears, has remembered the time, for when the picture comes clear we hear only the final strains of my theme song and what we see is a group of worried soldiers coming around a corner and slowing at the entrance to an old store. Nakamura's sign is banging in the early breeze and there is the added sound of artificial wind, something my producer made up to heighten the drama of the moment. The soldiers are unsure of themselves and thus give off a dangerous air. When they knock upon the door it is an expectation of trouble which comes through the screen and the viewers sit carefully forward to watch.

Alas, though I am not sorry that it will be seen, I cannot sit through the show myself. I stand while the others are settling, and opening the door to the Kado, slip quietly into the street. It is fine out here, cold but mild enough for walking. It seems impossible that only two weeks have passed since last I moved from the Kado to do my drinking in the larger bars. All of the pressures of the underworld were with me then but I had misdiagnosed them badly. Since then I have learned that what I am is only the tip of what there is and what tip does not follow the movements of the mass below?

I had thought to walk down the street a ways but I am stopped by the sound of the door opening behind me. Kazuko is on the street, hurrying to catch up and wrapping her shawl around her as she comes. I wait, fearing she might fall, and when she gets to me I take her arm in mine. "Come," I say, "we will have a drink in the seclusion of a place we do not know."

There is ice on the street, a fair chance of slipping, though I hadn't noticed it when I was alone. Roppongi is an area of the city where winter doesn't hinder activity, and as we arrive on the main street we find ourselves swept into the light and easy flow of the crowd. Quickly I look to see what tricks the glow from the Kado's light might play from such a distance, but there is nothing there. Kazuko nudges me. "I could work, upon occasion," she says, and it takes me a moment to realize that she is talking about maintaining the business of the bar.

When we come to the entrance to our son's favorite club I ask my wife if she'd like to go inside. But as always the bar is crowded, and there are two small lines of people at the door. While Kazuko and I wait, leaning against each other and moving a little in the cold air, a foreign-looking man comes around the corner and down the street toward us. When he gets precisely beside me he pauses and looks about him as if tentative and I speak to him without a thought.

"What is it that you are looking for?" I ask. "How is it that I might be of help?"

Kazuko is looking at the man with understanding in her eyes while he explains his dilemma to me. I am watching my wife's face carefully but listening to his every word. From his accent I can tell that he is American. From his story that he is utterly lost.

*